RAFFLES

The Amateur Cracksman

RAFFLES.

RAFFLES
The Amateur Cracksman

BY

Ernest William Hornung

ILLUSTRATED BY
F. C. Yohn

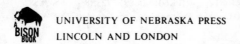

UNIVERSITY OF NEBRASKA PRESS
LINCOLN AND LONDON

The quotations in Part 2 of the Publisher's Preface are excerpted and reprinted by permission of Harcourt Brace Jovanovich, Inc. from "Raffles and Miss Blandish" in *Dickens, Dali and Others* by George Orwell, copyright, 1946, by George Orwell; copyright, 1974, by Sonia Orwell.

The University of Nebraska Press is grateful to Mrs. Sonia Brownell Orwell and to Martin Secker and Warburg Ltd. for their kind permission to reprint this material.

Originally published under the title *The Amateur Cracksman*

First Bison Book printing: 1976

Most recent printing indicated by the first digit below:
1   2   3   4   5   6   7   8   9   10

Library of Congress Cataloging in Publication Data
Hornung, Ernest William, 1866–1921.
    Raffles, the amateur cracksman.

    "A Bison book."
    Reprint, with new introd., of the 1899 ed. published by Scribner, New York.
    I. Title.
[PZ3.H786Raf12]   [PR6015.O687]   823'.8   75–38587
ISBN 0–8032–5836–4

Publisher's Preface

raffles . . . *often cap:* an amateur or gentleman burglar
Webster's Third International Dictionary

When E. W. Hornung published *The Amateur Cracksman,* the first volume of "the stories which gave a gentlemanly crook to the world and a new word to the language,"[1] the year was 1899 and Queen Victoria was still on the throne. Although no new Raffles books appeared after 1909, for the next three decades the legend of A. J. Raffles was kept alive by a succession of stage and screen stars, John Barrymore, Ronald Colman, and David Niven among them. By 1975, however, when the University of Nebraska Press began planning this edition of *The Amateur Cracksman,* thirty-five years had passed since the last motion-picture version of the exploits of Raffles and Bunny (his Boswell and partner in crime); and there seemed reason to suppose that they were casualties of World War II.

It has—happily—turned out otherwise. As this book goes to press, a play by Graham Greene, *The Return of A. J. Raffles,* is scheduled to open on Broadway following a successful London run.

Publisher's Preface

Thus, it seems in order to extend a welcome to this new incarnation of Raffles before presenting some biographical sidelights on Raffles's creator and a 1944 view of his creation by one of England's most astute social critics, the late George Orwell.

1

Ernest William Hornung was born on June 7, 1866, at Middlesborough, Yorkshire, and was educated at Uppingham—not by any means as fashionable as Eton or Harrow or Winchester, but ranked as one of the best of English public schools. Another future writer, Norman Douglas, who had a "slight personal acquaintance" with Hornung and who attended Uppingham during the same period, has left a singularly unenthusiastic picture of the school: the institution, he said, "reeked of Jeroboam and Jesus"; the masters struck him as "supercilious humbugs"; and "the herd-system and team life, congenial to many," went against his grain.[2] But, as Douglas recognized, "these things are a matter of temperament," and Hornung saw school life in quite a different light. That he absorbed and wholeheartedly subscribed to public-school values and the code of the old school tie is amply attested not only in the Raffles stories but also in his portrayal of Uppingham and its headmaster, Edward Thring, in *Fathers of Men* (1912), a novel which was hailed as "at once a fine tribute to a great school and a great master."[3]

After he left Uppingham in 1884, ill-health forced Hornung to go out to Australia; the two years he spent there provided him with material for several novels, including his first, *A Bride from the Bush* (1890). By 1891 he was well enough established as a popular writer to be among the first contributors to the sensationally successful *Strand Magazine*. In 1893 came his marriage to Constance Doyle, the sister of a fellow-contributor, A. Conan Doyle, whose *Strand* stories appeared in book form as *The Adventures of Sherlock Holmes*. Although six years passed before Hornung's Raffles and Bunny made their bow to the public, Doyle himself confirms that they were inspired by his own, far more famous fictional team. Recalling his brother-in-law in his autobiography, Doyle wrote that

Willie Hornung . . . was a Dr. Johnson without the learning but with a finer wit. No one could say a neater thing, and his writings, good as they are, never adequately represented the powers of the man, nor the quickness of his brain. . . . His criticism upon my Sherlock Holmes was: "Though he might be more humble, there is no police like Holmes." I think I may claim that his famous character Raffles was a kind of inversion of Sherlock Holmes, Bunny playing Watson. He admits as much in his kindly dedication. ["To A.C.D.: This form of flattery."] I think there are few finer examples of short-story writing in our language than these, though I confess I think they are rather dangerous in their suggestion. I told him so before he put pen to paper, and the result has, I fear, borne me out. You must not make the criminal a hero.[4]

Hornung is remembered today primarily for his Raffles books,[5] but he published some thirty other novels and short-story collections, mostly tales of adventure and detective stories. Representative titles are *The Boss of Taroomba* (1894), *Irralie's Bushranger* (1896), *Dead Men Tell No Tales* (1899), *The Shadow of the Rope* (1902), *No Hero* (1903), *The Camera Fiend* (1911), and *The Crime Doctor* (1914). The tales in *Stingaree* (1905) combine an Australian setting with a Raffles-like protagonist—a one-time London clubman who robs banks and the mails, and who chivalrously breaks the law to further the career of a young lady singer. Hornung also wrote *The Young Guard* (1919), a volume of war poems, and *Notes of a Camp-Follower on the Western Front* (1919), recollections of his experiences in France. His last book, *No Offenders* (1923), with a preface by Sir A. Conan Doyle, was published two years after his death on March 22, 1921. A reviewer of the posthumous volume, Hugh Caister, epitomized Hornung as a cricketer, a sentimentalist, and a craftsman. "He had, indeed, talents which in a generation less brilliant than his own might have commanded immediate respect, and which in any generation might, had he bothered, have been made the vehicle of great ideas. But he did not bother. Raffles came to him once, and he wrote a minor classic."[6]

2

George Orwell's view of Raffles was expressed in a 1944 essay, "Raffles and Miss Blandish,"[7] which compares a currently popular "version of glamorised crime," James Hadley Chase's *No Orchids for Miss Blandish* (1939), with the turn-of-the-century version, as exemplified by the Raffles books. Excerpts from Orwell's essay follow.

Nearly half a century after his first appearance, Raffles, "the amateur cracksman," is still one of the best-known characters in English fiction. Very few people would need telling that he played cricket for England, had bachelor chambers in the Albany and burgled the Mayfair houses which he also entered as a guest. . . .

At this date, the charm of *Raffles* is partly in the period atmosphere and partly in the technical excellence of the stories. Hornung was a very conscientious and on his level a very able writer. Anyone who cares for sheer efficiency must admire his work. However, the truly dramatic thing about Raffles, the thing that makes him sort of a byword even to this day (only a few weeks ago, in a burglary case, a magistrate referred to the prisoner as "a Raffles in real life"), is the fact that he is *a gentleman*. Raffles is presented to us—and this is rubbed home in countless scraps of dialogue and casual remarks—not as an honest man who has gone astray, but as a public-school man who has gone astray. His remorse, when he feels any, is almost purely social; he has disgraced "the old school," and has lost the right to enter "decent society," he has forfeited his amateur status and become a cad. Neither Raffles nor Bunny appears to feel at all strongly that stealing is wrong in itself, though Raffles does once justify himself by the casual remark that "the distribution of property is all wrong anyway." They think of themselves not as sinners but as renegades or simply outcasts. . . .

Raffles, of course, is good at all games, but it is peculiarly fitting that his chosen game should be cricket. This allows not only of endless analogies between his cunning as a slow bowler and his cunning as a burglar, but also helps to define the exact nature of his crime. Cricket is not in reality a very popular game in England—it is nowhere near so popular as football, for instance—but it gives expression to a well-marked trait in the British character, the tendency to value "form" or "style" more highly than success. In the eyes of any true cricket-lover it is possible for an innings of ten runs to be "better" (*i.e.* more elegant) than an innings of a hundred runs: cricket is also one of the very few games in which the amateur can excel the professional. It is a game full

Publisher's Preface

of forlorn hopes and sudden dramatic changes of fortune, and its rules are so ill-defined that their interpretation is partly an ethical business. . . . Since cricket takes up a lot of time and is rather an expensive game to play, it is predominantly an upper-class game, but for the whole nation it is bound up with such concepts as "good form," "playing the game," etc., and it has declined in popularity just as the tradition of "don't hit a man when he's down" has declined. It is not a twentieth-century game, and nearly all modern-minded people dislike it. . . . In making Raffles a cricketer as well as a burglar, Hornung was not merely providing him with a plausible disguise; he was also drawing the sharpest moral contrast that he was able to imagine.

Raffles, no less than *Great Expectations* or *Le Rouge et le Noir,* is a story of snobbery, and it gains a great deal from the precariousness of Raffles's social position. A cruder writer would have made the "gentleman burglar" a member of the peerage, or at least a baronet. Raffles, however, is of upper-middle-class origin and is only accepted by the aristocracy because of his personal charm. "We were in Society but not of it," he says to Bunny towards the end of the book; and "I was asked about for my cricket." Both he and Bunny accept the values of "Society" unquestioningly, and would settle down in it for good if only they could get away with a big enough haul. The ruin that constantly threatens them is all the blacker because they only doubtfully "belong." A duke who has served a prison sentence is still a duke, whereas a mere man about town, if once disgraced, ceases to be "about town" for evermore. . . .

Both Raffles and Bunny, of course, are devoid of religious belief, and they have no real ethical code,

Publisher's Preface

merely certain rules of behavior which they observe semi-instinctively....Certain things are "not done," and the idea of doing them hardly arises. Raffles will not, for example, abuse hospitality. He will commit a burglary in a house where he is staying as a guest, but the victim must be a fellow-guest and not the host. He will not commit murder,[8] and he avoids violence wherever possible and prefers to carry out his robberies unarmed. He regards friendship as sacred, and is chivalrous though not moral in his relations with women. He will take extra risks in the name of "sportsmanship," and sometimes even for aesthetic reasons. And, above all, he is intensely patriotic....

The Raffles stories, written from the angle of the criminal, are much less anti-social than many modern stories written from the angle of the detective. The main impression that they leave behind is boyishness. They belong to a time when people had standards, though they happened to be foolish standards. Their key phrase is "not done." The line that they draw between good and evil is as senseless as a Polynesian taboo, but at least, like the taboo, it has the advantage that everyone accepts it.

University of Nebraska Press

April 1976

NOTES

1. *New York Times,* 25 July 1930, p. 20.

2. Norman Douglas, *Looking Back: An Autobiographical Excursion* (New York: Harcourt, Brace and Company, 1934), pp. 44, 53.

3. *Spectator* (London), 10 February 1912.

4. Sir Arthur Conan Doyle, *Memories and Adventures* (Boston: Little, Brown, and Company, 1924), pp. 252–53.

5. The Raffles canon consists of three volumes of short stories and a novel. The first volume, *The Amateur Cracksman,* was published in England by Methuen in March 1899; the first American edition was published by Charles Scribner's Sons in the same year. As subsequent volumes appeared and Raffles's popularity grew, editions and reissues began to proliferate under the imprints of ten or more English, American, and German houses (exclusive of foreign-language editions). Variations in titles also began to occur, and without the actual volumes in hand it sometimes is impossible to determine which stories are included under a particular title. The list below specifies the stories which appeared in the first American editions, all published by Charles Scribner's Sons.

1899. *The Amateur Cracksman.* The eight tales in the present volume: "The Ides of March." "A Costume Piece." "Gentlemen and Players." "Le Premier Pas." "Wilful Murder." "Nine Points of the Law." "The Return Match." "The Gift of the Emperor."

1901. *Raffles: Further Adventures of the Amateur Cracksman.* Eight tales, the last of which describes Raffles's death in the Boer War. "No Sinecure." "A Jubilee Present." "The Fate of Faustina." "The Last Laugh." "To Catch a Thief." "An Old Flame." "The Wrong House." "The Knees of the Gods."

1905. *A Thief in the Night: Further Adventures of A. J. Raffles, Cricketer and Cracksman.* The tales in this volume go back to the earliest days of the Raffles-and-Bunny partnership. "Out of Paradise." "The Chest of Silver." "The Rest Cure." "The Criminologists' Club." "The Field of Philippi." "A Bad Night." "A Trap to Catch a Cracksman." "The Spoils of Sacrilege." "The Raffles Relics." "The Last Word."

1909. *Mr. Justice Raffles.* A novel describing Raffles's exploits in the course of seeing justice rendered to a young cricket player entrapped by a moneylender.

Notes

6. *Outlook* (London), 19 May 1923. Quoted in Stanley J. Kunitz and Howard Haycraft, *Twentieth Century Authors* (New York: H. W. Wilson Company, 1942), p. 667.

7. Collected in *Critical Essays* (London: Martin Secker and Warburg Ltd., 1946). The volume was published in the United States under the title *Dickens, Dali and Others* (New York: Reynal & Hitchcock, 1946).

8. [Note added by Orwell in 1945.] Actually Raffles does kill one man and is more or less consciously responsible for the death of two others. But all three of them are foreigners and have behaved in a very reprehensible manner. He also, on one occasion, contemplates murdering a blackmailer. It is, however, a fairly well-established convention in crime stories that murdering a blackmailer "doesn't count."

CONTENTS

ILLUSTRATIONS

The Amateur Cracksman

The Ides of March

I

IT was half-past twelve when I returned to the Albany as a last desperate resort. The scene of my disaster was much as I had left it. The baccarat-counters still strewed the table, with the empty glasses and the loaded ash-trays. A window had been opened to let the smoke out, and was letting in the fog instead. Raffles himself had merely discarded his dining jacket for one of his innumerable blazers. Yet he arched his eyebrows as though I had dragged him from his bed.

"Forgotten something?" said he, when he saw me on his mat.

"No," said I, pushing past him without ceremony. And I led the way into his room with an impudence amazing to myself.

"Not come back for your revenge, have you? Because I'm afraid I can't give it to you single-handed. I was sorry myself that the others——"

We were face to face by his fireside, and I cut him short.

"Raffles," said I, "you may well be surprised at my coming back in this way and at this hour. I hardly know you. I was never in your rooms before to-night. But I fagged for you at school, and you said you remembered me. Of course that's no excuse; but will you listen to me — for two minutes?"

In my emotion I had at first to struggle for every word; but his face reassured me as I went on, and I was not mistaken in its expression.

"Certainly, my dear man," said he; "as many minutes as you like. Have a Sullivan and sit down." And he handed me his silver cigarette-case.

"No," said I, finding a full voice as I shook my head; "no, I won't smoke, and I won't sit down, thank you. Nor will you ask me to do either when you've heard what I have to say."

"Really?" said he, lighting his own cigarette with one clear blue eye upon me. "How do you know?"

"Because you'll probably show me the door," I cried bitterly; "and you will be justified in doing it!

The Ides of March

But it's no use beating about the bush. You know I dropped over two hundred just now?"

He nodded.

"I hadn't the money in my pocket."

"I remember."

"But I had my check-book, and I wrote each of you a check at that desk."

"Well?"

"Not one of them was worth the paper it was written on, Raffles. I am overdrawn already at my bank!"

"Surely only for the moment?"

"No. I have spent everything."

"But somebody told me you were so well off. I heard you had come in for money?"

"So I did. Three years ago. It has been my curse; now it's all gone—every penny! Yes, I've been a fool; there never was nor will be such a fool as I've been. . . . Isn't this enough for you? Why don't you turn me out?" He was walking up and down with a very long face instead.

"Couldn't your people do anything?" he asked at length.

"Thank God," I cried, "I have no people! I was an only child. I came in for everything there was. My one comfort is that they're gone, and will never know."

3

The Amateur Cracksman

I cast myself into a chair and hid my face. Raffles continued to pace the rich carpet that was of a piece with everything else in his rooms. There was no variation in his soft and even footfalls.

"You used to be a literary little cuss," he said at length; "didn't you edit the mag. before you left? Anyway I recollect fagging you to do my verses; and literature of all sorts is the very thing nowadays; any fool can make a living at it."

I shook my head. "Any fool couldn't write off my debts," said I.

"Then you have a flat somewhere?" he went on.

"Yes, in Mount Street."

"Well, what about the furniture?"

I laughed aloud in my misery. "There's been a bill of sale on every stick for months!"

And at that Raffles stood still, with raised eyebrows and stern eyes that I could meet the better now that he knew the worst; then, with a shrug, he resumed his walk, and for some minutes neither of us spoke. But in his handsome, unmoved face I read my fate and death-warrant; and with every breath I cursed my folly and my cowardice in coming to him at all. Because he had been kind to me at school, when he was captain of the eleven, and I his fag, I had dared to look for kindness from him now; because I was ruined, and he rich enough

The Ides of March

to play cricket all the summer, and do nothing for the rest of the year, I had fatuously counted on his mercy, his sympathy, his help! Yes, I had relied on him in my heart, for all my outward diffidence and humility; and I was rightly served. There was as little of mercy as of sympathy in that curling nostril, that rigid jaw, that cold blue eye which never glanced my way. I caught up my hat. I blundered to my feet. I would have gone without a word; but Raffles stood between me and the door.

"Where are you going?" said he.

"That's my business," I replied. "I won't trouble *you* any more."

"Then how am I to help you?"

"I didn't ask your help."

"Then why come to me?"

"Why, indeed!" I echoed. "Will you let me pass?"

"Not until you tell me where you are going and what you mean to do."

"Can't you guess?" I cried. And for many seconds we stood staring in each other's eyes.

"Have you got the pluck?" said he, breaking the spell in a tone so cynical that it brought my last drop of blood to the boil.

"You shall see," said I, as I stepped back and

5

whipped the pistol from my overcoat pocket. "Now, will you let me pass or shall I do it here?"

The barrel touched my temple, and my thumb the trigger. Mad with excitement as I was, ruined, dishonored, and now finally determined to make an end of my misspent life, my only surprise to this day is that I did not do so then and there. The despicable satisfaction of involving another in one's destruction added its miserable appeal to my baser egoism; and had fear or horror flown to my companion's face, I shudder to think I might have died diabolically happy with that look for my last impious consolation. It was the look that came instead which held my hand. Neither fear nor horror were in it; only wonder, admiration, and such a measure of pleased expectancy as caused me after all to pocket my revolver with an oath.

"You devil!" I said. "I believe you wanted me to do it!"

"Not quite," was the reply, made with a little start, and a change of color that came too late. "To tell you the truth, though, I half thought you meant it, and I was never more fascinated in my life. I never dreamt you had such stuff in you, Bunny! No, I'm hanged if I let you go now. And you'd better not try that game again, for you won't catch me stand and look on a second time. We

must think of some way out of the mess. I had no
idea you were a chap of that sort! There, let me
have the gun."

One of his hands fell kindly on my shoulder,
while the other slipped into my overcoat pocket,
and I suffered him to deprive me of my weapon
without a murmur. Nor was this simply because
Raffles had the subtle power of making himself
irresistible at will. He was beyond comparison the
most masterful man whom I have ever known; yet
my acquiescence was due to more than the mere
subjection of the weaker nature to the stronger.
The forlorn hope which had brought me to the
Albany was turned as by magic into an almost
staggering sense of safety. Raffles would help me
after all! A. J. Raffles would be my friend! It
was as though all the world had come round suddenly to my side; so far therefore from resisting
his action, I caught and clasped his hand with a
fervor as uncontrollable as the frenzy which had
preceded it.

"God bless you!" I cried. "Forgive me for
everything. I will tell you the truth. I *did* think
you might help me in my extremity, though I well
knew that I had no claim upon you. Still—for the
old school's sake—the sake of old times—I
thought you might give me another chance. If you

wouldn't I meant to blow out my brains—and will still if you change your mind!"

In truth I feared that it was changing, with his expression, even as I spoke, and in spite of his kindly tone and kindlier use of my old school nickname. His next words showed me my mistake.

"What a boy it is for jumping to conclusions! I have my vices, Bunny, but backing and filling is not one of them. Sit down, my good fellow, and have a cigarette to soothe your nerves. I insist. Whiskey? The worst thing for you; here's some coffee that I was brewing when you came in. Now listen to me. You speak of 'another chance.' What do you mean? Another chance at baccarat? Not if I know it! You think the luck must turn; suppose it didn't? We should only have made bad worse. No, my dear chap, you've plunged enough. Do you put yourself in my hands or do you not? Very well, then you plunge no more, and I undertake not to present my check. Unfortunately there are the other men; and still more unfortunately, Bunny, I'm as hard up at this moment as you are yourself!"

It was my turn to stare at Raffles. "You?" I vociferated. "You hard up? How am I to sit here and believe that?"

"Did I refuse to believe it of you?" he returned,

smiling. "And, with your own experience, do you think that because a fellow has rooms in this place, and belongs to a club or two, and plays a little cricket, he must necessarily have a balance at the bank? I tell you, my dear man, that at this moment I'm as hard up as you ever were. I have nothing but my wits to live on—absolutely nothing else. It was as necessary for me to win some money this evening as it was for you. We're in the same boat, Bunny; we'd better pull together."

"Together!" I jumped at it. "I'll do anything in this world for you, Raffles," I said, "if you really mean that you won't give me away. Think of anything you like, and I'll do it! I was a desperate man when I came here, and I'm just as desperate now. I don't mind what I do if only I can get out of this without a scandal."

Again I see him, leaning back in one of the luxurious chairs with which his room was furnished. I see his indolent, athletic figure; his pale, sharp, clean-shaven features; his curly black hair; his strong, unscrupulous mouth. And again I feel the clear beam of his wonderful eye, cold and luminous as a star, shining into my brain—sifting the very secrets of my heart.

"I wonder if you mean all that!" he said at length. "You do in your present mood; but who can back his mood to last? Still, there's hope when a chap takes that tone. Now I think of it, too, you were a plucky little devil at school; you once did me rather a good turn, I recollect. Remember it, Bunny? Well, wait a bit, and perhaps I'll be able to do you a better one. Give me time to think."

He got up, lit a fresh cigarette, and fell to pacing the room once more, but with a slower and more thoughtful step, and for a much longer period than before. Twice he stopped at my chair as though on the point of speaking, but each time he checked himself and resumed his stride in silence. Once he threw up the window, which he had shut some time since, and stood for some moments leaning out into the fog which filled the Albany courtyard. Meanwhile a clock on the chimney-piece struck one, and one again for the half-hour, without a word between us.

Yet I not only kept my chair with patience, but I acquired an incongruous equanimity in that half-hour. Insensibly I had shifted my burden to the broad shoulders of this splendid friend, and my thoughts wandered with my eyes as the minutes passed. The room was the good-sized, square one, with the folding doors, the marble mantel-piece, and the gloomy, old-fashioned distinction peculiar to the Albany. It was charmingly furnished and arranged, with the right amount of negligence and the right amount of taste. What struck me most, however, was the absence of the usual insignia of a cricketer's den. Instead of the conventional rack of war-worn bats, a carved oak bookcase, with every shelf in a litter, filled the better part of one wall; and where I looked for cricketing groups, I found reproductions of such works as "Love and Death" and "The Blessed Damozel," in dusty frames and different parallels. The man might have been a minor poet instead of an athlete of the first water. But there had always been a fine streak of æstheticism in his complex composition; some of these very pictures I had myself dusted in his study at school; and they set me thinking of yet another of his many sides—and of the little incident to which he had just referred.

Everybody knows how largely the tone of a public school depends on that of the eleven, and on the character of the captain of cricket in particular; and I have never heard it denied that in A. J. Raffles's time our tone was good, or that such influence as he troubled to exert was on the side of the angels. Yet it was whispered in the school that he was in the habit of parading the town at night in loud checks and a false beard. It was whispered, and disbelieved. I alone knew it for a fact; for night after night had I pulled the rope up after him when the rest of the dormitory were asleep, and kept awake by the hour to let it down again on a given signal. Well, one night he was over-bold, and within an ace of ignominious expulsion in the hey-day of his fame. Consummate daring and extraordinary nerve on his part, aided, doubtless, by some little presence of mind on mine, averted the untoward result; and no more need be said of a discreditable incident. But I cannot pretend to have forgotten it in throwing myself on this man's mercy in my desperation. And I was wondering how much of his leniency was owing to the fact that Raffles had not forgotten it either, when he stopped and stood over my chair once more.

"I've been thinking of that night we had the narrow squeak," he began. "Why do you start?"

"I was thinking of it too."

He smiled, as though he had read my thoughts.

"Well, you were the right sort of little beggar then, Bunny; you didn't talk and you didn't flinch. You asked no questions and you told no tales. I wonder if you're like that now?"

"I don't know," said I, slightly puzzled by his tone. "I've made such a mess of my own affairs that I trust myself about as little as I'm likely to

The Ides of March

be trusted by anybody else. Yet I never in my life went back on a friend. I will say that, otherwise perhaps I mightn't be in such a hole to-night."

"Exactly," said Raffles, nodding to himself, as though in assent to some hidden train of thought; "exactly what I remember of you, and I'll bet it's as true now as it was ten years ago. We don't alter, Bunny. We only develop. I suppose neither you nor I are really altered since you used to let down that rope and I used to come up it hand over hand. You would stick at nothing for a pal—what?"

"At nothing in this world," I was pleased to cry.

"Not even at a crime?" said Raffles, smiling.

I stopped to think, for his tone had changed, and I felt sure he was chaffing me. Yet his eye seemed as much in earnest as ever, and for my part I was in no mood for reservations.

"No, not even at that," I declared; "name your crime, and I'm your man."

He looked at me one moment in wonder, and another moment in doubt; then turned the matter off with a shake of his head, and the little cynical laugh that was all his own.

"You're a nice chap, Bunny! A real desperate character—what? Suicide one moment, and any crime I like the next! What you want is a drag, my boy, and you did well to come to a decent law-abiding citizen with a reputation to lose. None the less we must have that money to-night—by hook or crook."

"To-night, Raffles?"

"The sooner the better. Every hour after ten o'clock to-morrow morning is an hour of risk. Let one of those checks get round to your own bank, and you and it are dishonored together. No, we must raise the wind to-night and re-open your account first thing to-morrow. And I rather think I know where the wind can be raised."

"At two o'clock in the morning?"

"Yes."

"But how—but where—at such an hour?"

"From a friend of mine here in Bond Street."

"He must be a very intimate friend!"

"Intimate's not the word. I have the run of his place and a latch-key all to myself."

"You would knock him up at this hour of the night?"

"If he's in bed."

"And it's essential that I should go in with you?"

"Absolutely."

"Then I must; but I'm bound to say I don't like the idea, Raffles."

"Do you prefer the alternative?" asked my com-

panion, with a sneer. "No, hang it, that's unfair!"
he cried apologetically in the same breath. "I
quite understand. It's a beastly ordeal. But it
would never do for you to stay outside. I tell you
what, you shall have a peg before we start—just
one. There's the whiskey, here's a syphon, and I'll
be putting on an overcoat while you help yourself."

Well, I daresay I did so with some freedom, for
this plan of his was not the less distasteful to me
from its apparent inevitability. I must own, however, that it possessed fewer terrors before my
glass was empty. Meanwhile Raffles rejoined me,
with a covert coat over his blazer, and a soft felt
hat set carelessly on the curly head he shook with
a smile as I passed him the decanter.

"When we come back," said he. "Work first,
play afterward. Do you see what day it is?" he
added, tearing a leaflet from a Shakespearian cal-
endar, as I drained my glass. "March 15th. 'The
Ides of March, the Ides of March, remember.'
Eh, Bunny, my boy? You won't forget them, will
you?"

And, with a laugh, he threw some coals on the
fire before turning down the gas like a careful
householder. So we went out together as the clock
on the chimney-piece was striking two.

The Amateur Cracksman

II

Piccadilly was a trench of raw white fog, rimmed with blurred street-lamps, and lined with a thin coating of adhesive mud. We met no other wayfarers on the deserted flagstones, and were ourselves favored with a very hard stare from the constable of the beat, who, however, touched his helmet on recognizing my companion.

"You see, I'm known to the police," laughed Raffles as we passed on. "Poor devils, they've got to keep their weather eye open on a night like this! A fog may be a bore to you and me, Bunny, but it's a perfect godsend to the criminal classes, especially so late in their season. Here we are, though— and I'm hanged if the beggar isn't in bed and asleep after all!"

We had turned into Bond Street, and had halted on the curb a few yards down on the right. Raffles was gazing up at some windows across the road, windows barely discernible through the mist, and without the glimmer of a light to throw them out. They were over a jeweller's shop, as I could see by the peep-hole in the shop door, and the bright light burning within. But the entire "upper part," with the private street-door next the shop, was black and blank as the sky itself.

"Better give it up for to-night," I urged. "Surely the morning will be time enough!"

"Not a bit of it," said Raffles. "I have his key. We'll surprise him. Come along."

And seizing my right arm, he hurried me across the road, opened the door with his latch-key, and in another moment had shut it swiftly but softly behind us. We stood together in the dark. Outside, a measured step was approaching; we had heard it through the fog as we crossed the street; now, as it drew nearer, my companion's fingers tightened on my arm.

"It may be the chap himself," he whispered. "He's the devil of a night-bird. Not a sound, Bunny! We'll startle the life out of him. Ah!"

The measured step had passed without a pause. Raffles drew a deep breath, and his singular grip of me slowly relaxed.

"But still, not a sound," he continued in the same whisper; "we'll take a rise out of him, wherever he is! Slip off your shoes and follow me."

Well, you may wonder at my doing so; but you can never have met A. J. Raffles. Half his power lay in a conciliating trick of sinking the commander in the leader. And it was impossible not to follow one who led with such a zest. You might question, but you followed first. So now, when I heard him kick off his own shoes, I did the same, and was on the stairs at his heels before I realized what an extraordinary way was this of approaching a stranger for money in the dead of night. But obviously Raffles and he were on exceptional terms of intimacy, and I could not but infer that they were in the habit of playing practical jokes upon each other.

We groped our way so slowly upstairs that I had time to make more than one note before we reached the top. The stair was uncarpeted. The spread fingers of my right hand encountered nothing on the damp wall; those of my left trailed through a dust that could be felt on the banisters. An eerie sensation had been upon me since we entered the house. It increased with every step we climbed. What hermit were we going to startle in his cell?

We came to a landing. The banisters led us to the left, and to the left again. Four steps more, and we were on another and a longer landing, and suddenly a match blazed from the black. I never heard it struck. Its flash was blinding. When my eyes became accustomed to the light, there was Raffles holding up the match with one hand, and shading it with the other, between bare boards, stripped walls, and the open doors of empty rooms.

"Where have you brought me?" I cried. "The house is unoccupied!"

"Hush! Wait!" he whispered, and he led the way into one of the empty rooms. His match went out as we crossed the threshold, and he struck another without the slightest noise. Then he stood with his back to me, fumbling with something that I could not see. But, when he threw the second match away, there was some other light in its stead, and a slight smell of oil. I stepped forward to look over his shoulder, but before I could do so he had turned and flashed a tiny lantern in my face.

"What's this?" I gasped. "What rotten trick are you going to play?"

"It's played," he answered, with his quiet laugh.

"On me?"

"I am afraid so, Bunny."

"Is there no one in the house, then?"

"No one but ourselves."

"So it was mere chaff about your friend in Bond Street, who could let us have that money?"

"Not altogether. It's quite true that Danby is a friend of mine."

"Danby?"

"The jeweller underneath."

"What do you mean?" I whispered, trembling like a leaf as his meaning dawned upon me. "Are we to get the money from the jeweller?"

"Well, not exactly."

"What, then?"

"The equivalent—from his shop."

There was no need for another question. I understood everything but my own density. He had given me a dozen hints, and I had taken none. And there I stood staring at him, in that empty room; and there he stood with his dark lantern, laughing at me.

"A burglar!" I gasped. "You—you!"

"I told you I lived by my wits."

"Why couldn't you tell me what you were going to do? Why couldn't you trust me? Why must you lie?" I demanded, piqued to the quick for all my horror.

"I wanted to tell you," said he. "I was on the point of telling you more than once. You may remember how I sounded you about crime, though you have probably forgotten what you said yourself. I didn't think you meant it at the time, but I thought I'd put you to the test. Now I see you didn't, and I don't blame you. I only am to blame. Get out of it, my dear boy, as quick as you can;

leave it to me. You won't give me away, whatever else you do!"

Oh, his cleverness! His fiendish cleverness! Had he fallen back on threats, coercion, sneers, all might have been different even yet. But he set me free to leave him in the lurch. He would not blame me. He did not even bind me to secrecy; he trusted me. He knew my weakness and my strength, and was playing on both with his master's touch.

"Not so fast," said I. "Did I put this into your head, or were you going to do it in any case?"

"Not in any case," said Raffles. "It's true I've had the key for days, but when I won to-night I thought of chucking it; for, as a matter of fact, it's not a one-man job."

"That settles it. I'm your man."

"You mean it?"

"Yes—for to-night."

"Good old Bunny," he murmured, holding the lantern for one moment to my face; the next he was explaining his plans, and I was nodding, as though we had been fellow-cracksmen all our days.

"I know the shop," he whispered, "because I've got a few things there. I know this upper part too; it's been to let for a month, and I got an order to view, and took a cast of the key before using it.

The Amateur Cracksman

The one thing I don't know is how to make a connection between the two; at present there's none. We may make it up here, though I rather fancy the basement myself. If you wait a minute I'll tell you."

He set his lantern on the floor, crept to a back window, and opened it with scarcely a sound: only to return, shaking his head, after shutting the window with the same care.

"That was our one chance," said he; "a back window above a back window; but it's too dark to see anything, and we daren't show an outside light. Come down after me to the basement; and remember, though there's not a soul on the premises, you can't make too little noise. There—there—listen to that!"

It was the measured tread that we had heard before on the flagstones outside. Raffles darkened his lantern, and again we stood motionless till it had passed.

"Either a policeman," he muttered, "or a watchman that all these jewellers run between them. The watchman's the man for us to watch; he's simply paid to spot this kind of thing."

We crept very gingerly down the stairs, which creaked a bit in spite of us, and we picked up our shoes in the passage; then down some narrow stone steps, at the foot of which Raffles showed his light, and put on his shoes once more, bidding me do the same in a rather louder tone than he had permitted himself to employ overhead. We were now considerably below the level of the street, in a small space with as many doors as it had sides. Three were ajar, and we saw through them into empty cellars; but in the fourth a key was turned and a bolt drawn; and this one presently let us out into the bottom of a deep, square well of fog. A similar door faced it across this area, and Raffles had the lantern close against it, and was hiding the light with his body, when a short and sudden crash made my heart stand still. Next moment I saw the door wide open, and Raffles standing within and beckoning me with a jimmy.

"Door number one," he whispered. "Deuce knows how many more there'll be, but I know of two at least. We won't have to make much noise over them, either; down here there's less risk."

We were now at the bottom of the exact fellow to the narrow stone stair which we had just descended: the yard, or well, being the one part common to both the private and the business premises. But this flight led to no open passage; instead, a singularly solid mahogany door confronted us at the top.

The Amateur Cracksman

"I thought so," muttered Raffles, handing me the lantern, and pocketing a bunch of skeleton keys, after tampering for a few minutes with the lock. "It'll be an hour's work to get through that!"

"Can't you pick it?"

"No. I know these locks. It's no use trying. We must cut it out, and it'll take us an hour."

It took us forty-seven minutes by my watch; or, rather, it took Raffles; and never in my life have I seen anything more deliberately done. My part was simply to stand by with the dark lantern in one hand, and a small bottle of rock-oil in the other. Raffles had produced a pretty embroidered case, intended obviously for his razors, but filled instead with the tools of his secret trade, including the rock-oil. From this case he selected a "bit," capable of drilling a hole an inch in diameter, and fitted it to a small but very strong steel "brace." Then he took off his covert-coat and his blazer, spread them neatly on the top step—knelt on them —turned up his shirt cuffs—and went to work with brace-and-bit near the key-hole. But first he oiled the bit to minimize the noise, and this he did invariably before beginning a fresh hole, and often in the middle of one. It took thirty-two separate borings to cut around that lock.

I noticed that through the first circular orifice

The Ides of March

Raffles thrust a forefinger; then, as the circle became an ever-lengthening oval, he got his hand through up to the thumb; and I heard him swear softly to himself.

"I was afraid so!"

"What is it?"

"An iron gate on the other side!"

"How on earth are we to get through that?" I asked in dismay.

"Pick the lock. But there may be two. In that case they'll be top and bottom, and we shall have two fresh holes to make, as the door opens inwards. It won't open two inches as it is."

I confess I did not feel sanguine about the lock-picking, seeing that one lock had baffled us already; and my disappointment and impatience must have been a revelation to me had I stopped to think. The truth is that I was entering into our nefarious undertaking with an involuntary zeal of which I was myself quite unconscious at the time. The romance and the peril of the whole proceeding held me spellbound and entranced. My moral sense and my sense of fear were stricken by a common paralysis. And there I stood, shining my light and holding my phial with a keener interest than I had ever brought to any honest avocation. And there knelt A. J. Raffles, with his black hair tumbled, and the same watchful, quiet, determined half-smile with which I have seen him send down over after over in a county match!

At last the chain of holes was complete, the lock wrenched out bodily, and a splendid bare arm plunged up to the shoulder through the aperture, and through the bars of the iron gate beyond.

"Now," whispered Raffles, "if there's only one lock it'll be in the middle. Joy! Here it is! Only let me pick it, and we're through at last."

He withdrew his arm, a skeleton key was selected from the bunch, and then back went his arm to the shoulder. It was a breathless moment. I heard the heart throbbing in my body, the very watch ticking in my pocket, and ever and anon the tinkle-tinkle of the skeleton key. Then—at last—there came a single unmistakable click. In another minute the mahogany door and the iron gate yawned behind us; and Raffles was sitting on an office table, wiping his face, with the lantern throwing a steady beam by his side.

We were now in a bare and roomy lobby behind the shop, but separated therefrom by an iron curtain, the very sight of which filled me with despair. Raffles, however, did not appear in the least depressed, but hung up his coat and hat on some pegs in the lobby before examining this curtain with his lantern.

"That's nothing," said he, after a minute's inspection; "we'll be through that in no time, but there's a door on the other side which may give us trouble."

"Another door!" I groaned. "And how do you mean to tackle this thing?"

"Prise it up with the jointed jimmy. The weak point of these iron curtains is the leverage you can get from below. But it makes a noise, and this is where you're coming in, Bunny; this is where I couldn't do without you. I must have you overhead to knock through when the street's clear. I'll come with you and show a light."

Well, you may imagine how little I liked the prospect of this lonely vigil; and yet there was something very stimulating in the vital responsibility which it involved. Hitherto I had been a mere spectator. Now I was to take part in the game. And the fresh excitement made me more than ever insensible to those considerations of conscience and of safety which were already as dead nerves in my breast.

So I took my post without a murmur in the front room above the shop. The fixtures had been left for the refusal of the incoming tenant, and fortunately for us they included Venetian blinds which were already down. It was the simplest matter in the world to stand peeping through the laths into the street, to beat twice with my foot when anybody was approaching, and once when all was clear again. The noises that even I could hear below, with the exception of one metallic crash at the beginning, were indeed incredibly slight; but they ceased altogether at each double rap from my toe; and a policeman passed quite half a dozen times beneath my eyes, and the man whom I took to be the jeweller's watchman oftener still, during the better part of an hour that I spent at the window. Once, indeed, my heart was in my mouth, but only once. It was when the watchman stopped and peered through the peep-hole into the lighted shop. I waited for his whistle—I waited for the gallows or the gaol! But my signals had been studiously obeyed, and the man passed on in undisturbed serenity. In the end I had a signal in my turn, and retraced my steps with lighted matches, down the broad stairs, down the narrow ones, across the area, and up into the lobby where Raffles awaited me with an outstretched hand.

"Well done, my boy!" said he. "You're the same good man in a pinch, and you shall have your reward. I've got a thousand pounds' worth if I've

got a penn'oth. It's all in my pockets. And here's
something else I found in this locker; very decent
port and some cigars, meant for poor dear Danby's
business friends. Take a pull, and you shall light
up presently. I've found a lavatory, too, and we
must have a wash-and-brush-up before we go, for
I'm as black as your boot."

The iron curtain was down, but he insisted on
raising it until I could peep through the glass door
on the other side and see his handiwork in the shop
beyond. Here two electric lights were left burning all night long, and in their cold white rays I
could at first see nothing amiss. I looked along
an orderly lane, an empty glass counter on my left,
glass cupboards of untouched silver on my right,
and facing me the filmy black eye of the peep-hole
that shone like a stage moon on the street. The
counter had not been emptied by Raffles; its contents were in the Chubb's safe, which he had given
up at a glance; nor had he looked at the silver,
except to choose a cigarette case for me. He had
confined himself entirely to the shop window. This
was in three compartments, each secured for the
night by removable panels with separate locks.
Raffles had removed them a few hours before their
time, and the electric light shone on a corrugated
shutter bare as the ribs of an empty carcase. Every

article of value was gone from the one place which was invisible from the little window in the door; elsewhere all was as it had been left overnight. And but for a train of mangled doors behind the iron curtain, a bottle of wine and a cigar-box with which liberties had been taken, a rather black towel in the lavatory, a burnt match here and there, and our finger-marks on the dusty banisters, not a trace of our visit did we leave.

"Had it in my head for long?" said Raffles, as we strolled through the streets towards dawn, for all the world as though we were returning from a dance. "No, Bunny, I never thought of it till I saw that upper part empty about a month ago, and bought a few things in the shop to get the lie of the land. That reminds me that I never paid for them; but, by Jove, I will to-morrow, and if that isn't poetic justice, what is? One visit showed me the possibilities of the place, but a second convinced me of its impossibilities without a pal. So I had practically given up the idea, when you came along on the very night and in the very plight for it! But here we are at the Albany, and I hope there's some fire left; for I don't know how you feel, Bunny, but for my part I'm as cold as Keats's owl."

He could think of Keats on his way from a fel-

The Ides of March

ony! He could hanker for his fireside like another! Floodgates were loosed within me, and the plain English of our adventure rushed over me as cold as ice. Raffles was a burglar. I had helped him to commit one burglary, therefore I was a burglar, too. Yet I could stand and warm myself by his fire, and watch him empty his pockets, as though we had done nothing wonderful or wicked!

My blood froze. My heart sickened. My brain whirled. How I had liked this villain! How I had admired him! Now my liking and admiration must turn to loathing and disgust. I waited for the change. I longed to feel it in my heart. But —I longed and I waited in vain!

I saw that he was emptying his pockets; the table sparkled with their hoard. Rings by the dozen, diamonds by the score; bracelets, pendants, aigrettes, necklaces, pearls, rubies, amethysts, sapphires; and diamonds always, diamonds in everything, flashing bayonets of light, dazzling me—blinding me—making me disbelieve because I could no longer forget. Last of all came no gem, indeed, but my own revolver from an inner pocket. And that struck a chord. I suppose I said something—my hand flew out. I can see Raffles now, as he looked at me once more with a high arch over each clear eye. I can see him pick out the cartridges with his quiet, cynical smile, before he would give me my pistol back again.

"You mayn't believe it, Bunny," said he, "but I never carried a loaded one before. On the whole I think it gives one confidence. Yet it would be very awkward if anything went wrong; one might use it, and that's not the game at all, though I have often thought that the murderer who has just done the trick must have great sensations before things get too hot for him. Don't look so distressed, my dear chap. I've never had those sensations, and I don't suppose I ever shall."

"But this much you have done before?" said I hoarsely.

"Before? My dear Bunny, you offend me! Did it look like a first attempt? Of course I have done it before."

"Often?"

"Well—no! Not often enough to destroy the charm, at all events; never, as a matter of fact, unless I'm cursedly hard up. Did you hear about the Thimbleby diamonds? Well, that was the last time—and a poor lot of paste they were. Then there was the little business of the Dormer house-boat at Henley last year. That was mine also—such as it was. I've never brought off a really big coup yet; when I do I shall chuck it up."

The Ides of March

Yes, I remembered both cases very well. To think that he was their author! It was incredible, outrageous, inconceivable. Then my eyes would fall upon the table, twinkling and glittering in a hundred places, and incredulity was at an end.

"How came you to begin?" I asked, as curiosity overcame mere wonder, and a fascination for his career gradually wove itself into my fascination for the man.

"Ah! that's a long story," said Raffles. "It was in the Colonies, when I was out there playing cricket. It's too long a story to tell you now, but I was in much the same fix that you were in to-night, and it was my only way out. I never meant it for anything more; but I'd tasted blood, and it was all over with me. Why should I work when I could steal? Why settle down to some humdrum uncongenial billet, when excitement, romance, danger and a decent living were all going begging together? Of course it's very wrong, but we can't all be moralists, and the distribution of wealth is very wrong to begin with. Besides, you're not at it all the time. I'm sick of quoting Gilbert's lines to myself, but they're profoundly true. I only wonder if you'll like the life as much as I do!"

"Like it?" I cried out. "Not I! It's no life for me. Once is enough!"

The Amateur Cracksman

"You wouldn't give me a hand another time?"

"Don't ask me, Raffles. Don't ask me, for God's sake!"

"Yet you said you would do anything for me! You asked me to name my crime! But I knew at the time you didn't mean it; you didn't go back on me to-night, and that ought to satisfy me, goodness knows! I suppose I'm ungrateful, and unreasonable, and all that. I ought to let it end at this. But you're the very man for me, Bunny, the—very—man! Just think how we got through to-night. Not a scratch—not a hitch! There's nothing very terrible in it, you see; there never would be, while we worked together."

He was standing in front of me with a hand on either shoulder; he was smiling as he knew so well how to smile. I turned on my heel, planted my elbows on the chimney-piece, and my burning head between my hands. Next instant a still heartier hand had fallen on my back.

"All right, my boy! You are quite right and I'm worse than wrong. I'll never ask it again. Go, if you want to, and come again about mid-day for the cash. There was no bargain; but, of course, I'll get you out of your scrape—especially after the way you've stood by me to-night."

I was round again with my blood on fire.

The Ides of March

"I'll do it again," I said, through my teeth.

He shook his head. "Not you," he said, smiling quite good-humoredly on my insane enthusiasm.

"I will," I cried with an oath. "I'll lend you a hand as often as you like! What does it matter now? I've been in it once. I'll be in it again. I've gone to the devil anyhow. I can't go back, and wouldn't if I could. Nothing matters another rap! When you want me, I'm your man!"

And that is how Raffles and I joined felonious forces on the Ides of March.

A Costume Piece

L ONDON was just then talking of one whose
name is already a name and nothing more.
Reuben Rosenthall had made his millions on the
diamond fields of South Africa, and had come home
to enjoy them according to his lights; how he went
to work will scarcely be forgotten by any reader of
the halfpenny evening papers, which revelled in
endless anecdotes of his original indigence and
present prodigality, varied with interesting partic-
ulars of the extraordinary establishment which the
millionaire set up in St. John's Wood. Here he
kept a retinue of Kaffirs, who were literally his
slaves; and hence he would sally, with enormous
diamonds in his shirt and on his finger, in the con-
voy of a prize-fighter of heinous repute, who was
not, however, by any means the worst element in
the Rosenthall *mélange*. So said common gossip;
but the fact was sufficiently established by the interference of the police on at least one occasion, followed by certain magisterial proceedings which
were reported with justifiable gusto and huge headlines in the newspapers aforesaid. And this was

A Costume Piece

all one knew of Reuben Rosenthall up to the time when the Old Bohemian Club, having fallen on evil days, found it worth its while to organize a great dinner in honor of so wealthy an exponent of the club's principles. I was not at the banquet myself, but a member took Raffles, who told me all about it that very night.

"Most extraordinary show I ever went to in my life," said he. "As for the man himself—well, I was prepared for something grotesque, but the fellow fairly took my breath away. To begin with, he's the most astounding brute to look at, well over six feet, with a chest like a barrel, and a great hook-nose, and the reddest hair and whiskers you ever saw. Drank like a fire-engine, but only got drunk enough to make us a speech that I wouldn't have missed for ten pounds. I'm only sorry you weren't there, too, Bunny, old chap."

I began to be sorry myself, for Raffles was anything but an excitable person, and never had I seen him so excited before. Had he been following Rosenthall's example? His coming to my rooms at midnight, merely to tell me about his dinner, was in itself enough to excuse a suspicion which was certainly at variance with my knowledge of A. J. Raffles.

"What did he say?" I inquired mechanically,

divining some subtler explanation of this visit, and wondering what on earth it could be.

"Say?" cried Raffles. "What did he not say! He boasted of his rise, he bragged of his riches, and he blackguarded society for taking him up for his money and dropping him out of sheer pique and jealousy because he had so much. He mentioned names, too, with the most charming freedom, and swore he was as good a man as the Old Country had to show—*pace* the Old Bohemians. To prove it he pointed to a great diamond in the middle of his shirt-front with a little finger loaded with another just like it: which of our bloated princes could show a pair like that? As a matter of fact, they seemed quite wonderful stones, with a curious purple gleam to them that must mean a pot of money. But old Rosenthall swore he wouldn't take fifty thousand pounds for the two, and wanted to know where the other man was who went about with twenty-five thousand in his shirt-front, and another twenty-five on his little finger. He didn't exist. If he did, he wouldn't have the pluck to wear them. But *he* had—he'd tell us why. And before you could say Jack Robinson he had whipped out a whacking great revolver!"

"Not at the table?"

"At the table! In the middle of his speech!

A Costume Piece

But it was nothing to what he wanted to do. He actually wanted us to let him write his name in bullets on the opposite wall, to show us why he wasn't afraid to go about in all his diamonds! That brute Purvis, the prize-fighter, who is his paid bully, had to bully his master before he could be persuaded out of it. There was quite a panic for the moment; one fellow was saying his prayers under the table, and the waiters bolted to a man."

"What a grotesque scene!"

"Grotesque enough, but I rather wish they had let him go the whole hog and blaze away. He was as keen as knives to show us how he could take care of his purple diamonds; and, do you know, Bunny, *I* was as keen as knives to see."

And Raffles leaned towards me with a sly, slow smile that made the hidden meaning of his visit only too plain to me at last.

"So you think of having a try for his diamonds yourself?"

He shrugged his shoulders.

"It is horribly obvious, I admit. But—yes, I have set my heart upon them! To be quite frank, I have had them on my conscience for some time; one couldn't hear so much of the man, and his prize-fighter, and his diamonds, without feeling it a kind of duty to have a go for them; but when it comes to brandishing a revolver and practically challenging the world, the thing becomes inevitable. It is simply thrust upon one. I was fated to hear that challenge, Bunny, and I, for one, must take it up. I was only sorry I couldn't get on my hind legs and say so then and there."

"Well," I said, "I don't see the necessity as things are with us; but, of course, I'm your man."

My tone may have been half-hearted. I did my best to make it otherwise. But it was barely a month since our Bond Street exploit, and we certainly could have afforded to behave ourselves for some time to come. We had been getting along so nicely: by his advice I had scribbled a thing or two; inspired by Raffles, I had even done an article on our own jewel robbery; and for the moment I was quite satisfied with this sort of adventure. I thought we ought to know when we were well off, and could see no point in our running fresh risks before we were obliged. On the other hand, I was anxious not to show the least disposition to break the pledge that I had given a month ago. But it was not on my manifest disinclination that Raffles fastened.

"Necessity, my dear Bunny? Does the writer only write when the wolf is at the door? Does the painter paint for bread alone? Must you and

A Costume Piece

I be *driven* to crime like Tom of Bow and Dick of Whitechapel? You pain me, my dear chap; you needn't laugh, because you do. Art for art's sake is a vile catchword, but I confess it appeals to me. In this case my motives are absolutely pure, for I doubt if we shall ever be able to dispose of such peculiar stones. But if I don't have a try for them —after to-night—I shall never be able to hold up my head again."

His eye twinkled, but it glittered, too.

"We shall have our work cut out," was all I said.

"And do you suppose I should be keen on it if we hadn't?" cried Raffles. "My dear fellow, I would rob St. Paul's Cathedral if I could, but I could no more scoop a till when the shopwalker wasn't looking than I could bag the apples out of an old woman's basket. Even that little business last month was a sordid affair, but it was necessary, and I think its strategy redeemed it to some extent. Now there's some credit, and more sport, in going where they boast they're on their guard against you. The Bank of England, for example, is the ideal crib; but that would need half a dozen of us with years to give to the job; and meanwhile Reuben Rosenthall is high enough game for you and me. We know he's armed. We know how Billy

Purvis can fight. It'll be no soft thing, I grant you. But what of that, my good Bunny—what of that? A man's reach must exceed his grasp, dear boy, or what the dickens is a heaven for?"

"I would rather we didn't exceed ours just yet," I answered laughing, for his spirit was irresistible, and the plan was growing upon me, despite my qualms.

"Trust me for that," was his reply; "I'll see you through. After all I expect to find that the difficulties are nearly all on the surface. These fellows both drink like the devil, and that should simplify matters considerably. But we shall see, and we must take our time. There will probably turn out to be a dozen different ways in which the thing might be done, and we shall have to choose between them. It will mean watching the house for at least a week in any case; it may mean lots of other things that will take much longer; but give me a week and I will tell you more. That's to say, if you're really on?"

"Of course I am," I replied indignantly. "But why should I give you a week? Why shouldn't we watch the house together?"

"Because two eyes are as good as four and take up less room. Never hunt in couples unless you're obliged. But don't you look offended, Bunny;

there'll be plenty for you to do when the time comes, that I promise you. You shall have your share of the fun, never fear, and a purple diamond all to yourself—if we're lucky."

On the whole, however, this conversation left me less than lukewarm, and I still remember the depression which came upon me when Raffles was gone. I saw the folly of the enterprise to which I had committed myself—the sheer, gratuitous, unnecessary folly of it. And the paradoxes in which Raffles revelled, and the frivolous casuistry which was nevertheless half sincere, and which his mere personality rendered wholly plausible at the moment of utterance, appealed very little to me when recalled in cold blood. I admired the spirit of pure mischief in which he seemed prepared to risk his liberty and his life, but I did not find it an infectious spirit on calm reflection. Yet the thought of withdrawal was not to be entertained for a moment. On the contrary, I was impatient of the delay ordained by Raffles; and, perhaps, no small part of my secret disaffection came of his galling determination to do without me until the last moment.

It made it no better that this was characteristic of the man and of his attitude towards me. For a month we had been, I suppose, the thickest thieves in all London, and yet our intimacy was curiously incomplete. With all his charming frankness, there was in Raffles a vein of capricious reserve which was perceptible enough to be very irritating. He had the instinctive secretiveness of the inveterate criminal. He would make mysteries of matters of common concern; for example, I never knew how or where he disposed of the Bond Street jewels, on the proceeds of which we were both still leading the outward lives of hundreds of other young fellows about town. He was consistently mysterious about that and other details, of which it seemed to me that I had already earned the right to know everything. I could not but remember how he had led me into my first felony, by means of a trick, while yet uncertain whether he could trust me or not. That I could no longer afford to resent, but I did resent his want of confidence in me now. I said nothing about it, but it rankled every day, and never more than in the week that succeeded the Rosenthall dinner. When I met Raffles at the club he would tell me nothing; when I went to his rooms he was out, or pretended to be.

One day he told me he was getting on well, but slowly; it was a more ticklish game than he had thought; but when I began to ask questions he would say no more. Then and there, in my annoyance, I took my own decision. Since he would tell me nothing of the result of his vigils, I determined to keep one on my own account, and that very evening found my way to the millionaire's front gates.

The house he was occupying is, I believe, quite the largest in the St. John's Wood district. It stands in the angle formed by two broad thoroughfares, neither of which, as it happens, is a 'bus route, and I doubt if many quieter spots exist within the four-mile radius. Quiet also was the great square house, in its garden of grass-plots and shrubs; the lights were low, the millionaire and his friends obviously spending their evening elsewhere. The garden walls were only a few feet high. In one there was a side door opening into a glass passage; in the other two five-barred, grained-and-varnished gates, one at either end of the little semi-circular drive, and both wide open. So still was the place that I had a great mind to walk boldly in and learn something of the premises; in fact, I was on the point of doing so, when I heard a quick, shuffling step on the pavement behind me. I turned round and faced the dark scowl and the dirty clenched fists of a dilapidated tramp.

"You fool!" said he. "You utter idiot!"

"Raffles!"

The Amateur Cracksman

"That's it," he whispered savagely; "tell all the neighborhood—give me away at the top of your voice!"

With that he turned his back upon me, and shambled down the road, shrugging his shoulders and muttering to himself as though I had refused him alms. A few moments I stood astounded, indignant, at a loss; then I followed him. His feet trailed, his knees gave, his back was bowed, his head kept nodding; it was the gait of a man eighty years of age. Presently he waited for me midway between two lamp-posts. As I came up he was lighting rank tobacco, in a cutty pipe, with an evil-smelling match, and the flame showed me the suspicion of a smile.

"You must forgive my heat, Bunny, but it really was very foolish of you. Here am I trying every dodge—begging at the door one night—hiding in the shrubs the next—doing every mortal thing but stand and stare at the house as you went and did. It's a costume piece, and in you rush in your ordinary clothes. I tell you they're on the lookout for us night and day. It's the toughest nut I ever tackled!"

"Well," said I, "if you had told me so before I shouldn't have come. You told me nothing."

A Costume Piece

He looked hard at me from under the broken brim of a battered billycock.

"You're right," he said at length. "I've been too close. It's become second nature with me when I've anything on. But here's an end of it, Bunny, so far as you're concerned. I'm going home now, and I want you to follow me; but for heaven's sake keep your distance, and don't speak to me again till I speak to you. There—give me a start." And he was off again, a decrepit vagabond, with his hands in his pockets, his elbows squared, and frayed coat-tails swinging raggedly from side to side.

I followed him to the Finchley Road. There he took an Atlas omnibus, and I sat some rows behind him on the top, but not far enough to escape the pest of his vile tobacco. That he could carry his character-sketch to such a pitch—he who would only smoke one brand of cigarette! It was the last, least touch of the insatiable artist, and it charmed away what mortification there still remained in me. Once more I felt the fascination of a comrade who was forever dazzling one with a fresh and unsuspected facet of his character.

As we neared Piccadilly I wondered what he would do. Surely he was not going into the Albany like that? No, he took another omnibus to Sloane Street, I sitting behind him as before. At Sloane

Street we changed again, and were presently in the long lean artery of the King's Road. I was now all agog to know our destination, nor was I kept many more minutes in doubt. Raffles got down. I followed. He crossed the road and disappeared up a dark turning. I pressed after him, and was in time to see his coat-tails as he plunged into a still darker flagged alley to the right. He was holding himself up and stepping out like a young man once more; also, in some subtle way, he already looked less disreputable. But I alone was there to see him, the alley was absolutely deserted, and desperately dark. At the further end he opened a door with a latch-key, and it was darker yet within.

Instinctively I drew back and heard him chuckle. We could no longer see each other.

"All right, Bunny! There's no hanky-panky this time. These are studios, my friend, and I'm one of the lawful tenants."

Indeed, in another minute we were in a lofty room with skylight, easels, dressing-cupboard, platform, and every other adjunct save the signs of actual labor. The first thing I saw, as Raffles lit the gas, was its reflection in his silk hat on the pegs beside the rest of his normal garments.

"Looking for the works of art?" continued Raffles, lighting a cigarette and beginning to divest

A Costume Piece

himself of his rags. "I'm afraid you won't find any, but there's the canvas I'm always going to make a start upon. I tell them I'm looking high and low for my ideal model. I have the stove lit on principle twice a week, and look in and leave a newspaper and a smell of Sullivans—how good they are after shag! Meanwhile I pay my rent and am a good tenant in every way; and it's a very useful little *pied-à-terre*—there's no saying how useful it might be at a pinch. As it is, the billy-cock comes in and the topper goes out, and nobody takes the slightest notice of either; at this time of night the chances are that there's not a soul in the building except ourselves."

"You never told me you went in for disguises," said I, watching him as he cleansed the grime from his face and hands.

"No, Bunny, I've treated you very shabbily all round. There was really no reason why I shouldn't have shown you this place a month ago, and yet there was no point in my doing so, and circumstances are just conceivable in which it would have suited us both for you to be in genuine ignorance of my whereabouts. I have something to sleep on, as you perceive, in case of need, and, of course, my name is not Raffles in the King's Road. So you will see that one might bolt further and fare worse."

The Amateur Cracksman

"Meanwhile you use the place as a dressing-room?"

"It is my private pavilion," said Raffles. "Disguises? In some cases they're half the battle, and it's always pleasant to feel that, if the worst comes to the worst, you needn't necessarily be convicted under your own name. Then they're indispensable in dealing with the fences. I drive all my bargains in the tongue and raiment of Shoreditch. If I didn't there'd be the very devil to pay in blackmail. Now, this cupboard's full of all sorts of toggery. I tell the woman who cleans the room that it's for my models when I find 'em. By the way, I only hope I've got something that'll fit you, for you'll want a rig for to-morrow night."

"To-morrow night!" I exclaimed. "Why, what do you mean to do?"

"The trick," said Raffles. "I intended writing to you as soon as I got back to my rooms, to ask you to look me up to-morrow afternoon; then I was going to unfold my plan of campaign, and take you straight into action then and there. There's nothing like putting the nervous players in first; it's the sitting with their pads on that upsets their applecart; that was another of my reasons for being so confoundedly close. You must try to forgive me. I couldn't help remembering how

50

well you played up last trip, without any time to weaken on it beforehand. All I want is for you to be as cool and smart to-morrow night as you were then; though, by Jove, there's no comparison between the two cases!"

"I thought you would find it so."

"You were right. I have. Mind you, I don't say this will be the tougher job all round; we shall probably get in without any difficulty at all; it's the getting out again that may flummox us. That's the worst of an irregular household!" cried Raffles, with quite a burst of virtuous indignation. "I assure you, Bunny, I spent the whole of Monday night in the shrubbery of the garden next door, looking over the wall, and, if you'll believe me, somebody was about all night long! I don't mean the Kaffirs. I don't believe they ever get to bed at all—poor devils! No, I mean Rosenthall himself, and that pasty-faced beast Purvis. They were up and drinking from midnight, when they came in, to broad daylight, when I cleared out. Even then I left them sober enough to slang each other. By the way, they very nearly came to blows in the garden, within a few yards of me, and I heard something that might come in useful and make Rosenthall shoot crooked at a critical moment. You know what an I. D. B. is?"

The Amateur Cracksman

"Illicit Diamond Buyer?"

"Exactly. Well, it seems that Rosenthall was one. He must have let it out to Purvis in his cups. Anyhow, I heard Purvis taunting him with it, and threatening him with the breakwater at Capetown; and I begin to think our friends are friend and foe. But about to-morrow night: there's nothing subtle in my plan. It's simply to get in while these fellows are out on the loose, and to lie low till they come back, and longer. If possible, we must doctor the whiskey. That would simplify the whole thing, though it's not a very sporting game to play; still, we must remember Rosenthall's revolver; we don't want him to sign his name on *us*. With all those Kaffirs about, however, it's ten to one on the whiskey, and a hundred to one against us if we go looking for it. A brush with the heathen would spoil everything, if it did no more. Besides, there are the ladies——"

"The deuce there are!"

"Ladies with an *i*, and the very voices for raising Cain. I fear, I fear the clamor! It would be fatal to us. *Au contraire*, if we can manage to stow ourselves away unbeknowns, half the battle will be won. If Rosenthall turns in drunk, it's a purple diamond apiece. If he sits up sober, it may be a bullet instead. We will hope not, Bunny:

A Costume Piece

and all the firing wouldn't be on one side; but it's on the knees of the gods."

And so we left it when we shook hands in Piccadilly—not by any means as much later as I could have wished. Raffles would not ask me to his rooms that night. He said he made it a rule to have a long night before playing cricket and—other games. His final word to me was framed on the same principle.

"Mind, only one drink to-night, Bunny. Two at the outside—as you value your life—and mine!"

I remember my abject obedience; and the endless, sleepless night it gave me; and the roofs of the houses opposite standing out at last against the blue-gray London dawn. I wondered whether I should ever see another, and was very hard on myself for that little expedition which I had made on my own wilful account.

It was between eight and nine o'clock in the evening when we took up our position in the garden adjoining that of Reuben Rosenthall; the house itself was shut up, thanks to the outrageous libertine next door, who, by driving away the neighbors, had gone far towards delivering himself into our hands. Practically secure from surprise on that side, we could watch our house under cover of a wall just high enough to see over, while a fair margin of shrubs in either garden afforded us additional protection. Thus entrenched, we had stood an hour, watching a pair of lighted bow-windows with vague shadows flitting continually across the blinds, and listening to the drawing of corks, the clink of glasses, and a gradual crescendo of coarse voices within. Our luck seemed to have deserted us: the owner of the purple diamonds was dining at home and dining at undue length. I thought it was a dinner-party. Raffles differed; in the end he proved right. Wheels grated in the drive, a carriage and pair stood at the steps; there was a stampede from the dining-room, and the loud voices died away, to burst forth presently from the porch.

Let me make our position perfectly clear. We were over the wall, at the side of the house, but a few feet from the dining-room windows. On our right, one angle of the building cut the back lawn in two diagonally; on our left, another angle just permitted us to see the jutting steps and the waiting carriage. We saw Rosenthall come out—saw the glimmer of his diamonds before anything. Then came the pugilist; then a lady with a head of hair like a bath sponge; then another, and the party was complete.

A Costume Piece

Raffles ducked and pulled me down in great excitement.

"The ladies are going with them," he whispered. "This is great!"

"That's better still."

"The Gardenia!" the millionaire had bawled.

"And that's best of all," said Raffles, standing upright as hoofs and wheels crunched through the gates and rattled off at a fine speed.

"Now what?" I whispered, trembling with excitement.

"They'll be clearing away. Yes, here come their shadows. The drawing-room windows open on the lawn. Bunny, it's the psychological moment. Where's that mask?"

I produced it with a hand whose trembling I tried in vain to still, and could have died for Raffles when he made no comment on what he could not fail to notice. His own hands were firm and cool as he adjusted my mask for me, and then his own.

"By Jove, old boy," he whispered cheerily, "you look about the greatest ruffian I ever saw! These masks alone will down a nigger, if we meet one. But I'm glad I remembered to tell you not to shave. You'll pass for Whitechapel if the worst comes to the worst and you don't forget to talk the lingo. Better sulk like a mule if you're not sure of it, and leave the dialogue to me; but, please our stars, there will be no need. Now, are you ready?"

"Quite."

"Got your gag?"

"Yes."

"Shooter?"

"Yes."

"Then follow me."

In an instant we were over the wall, in another on the lawn behind the house. There was no moon. The very stars in their courses had veiled themselves for our benefit. I crept at my leader's heels to some French windows opening upon a shallow veranda. He pushed. They yielded.

"Luck again," he whispered; "nothing *but* luck! Now for a light."

And the light came!

A good score of electric burners glowed red for the fraction of a second, then rained merciless white beams into our blinded eyes. When we found our sight four revolvers covered us, and between two of them the colossal frame of Reuben Rosenthall shook with a wheezy laughter from head to foot.

"Good-evening, boys," he hiccoughed. "Glad to see ye at last. Shift foot or finger, you on the left, though, and you're a dead boy. I mean you,

A Costume Piece

you greaser!" he roared out at Raffles. "I know you. I've been waitin' for you. I've been *watchin'* you all this week! Plucky smart you thought yerself, didn't you? One day beggin', next time shammin' tight, and next one o' them old pals from Kimberley what never come when I'm in. But you left the same tracks every day, you buggins, an' the same tracks every night, all round the blessed premises."

"All right, guv'nor," drawled Raffles; "don't excite. It's a fair cop. We don't sweat to know 'ow you brung it orf. On'y don't you go for to shoot, 'cos we 'int awmed, s'help me Gord!"

"Ah, you're a knowin' one," said Rosenthall, fingering his triggers. "But you've struck a knowin'er."

"Ho, yuss, we know all abaht thet! Set a thief to ketch a thief—ho, yuss."

My eyes had torn themselves from the round black muzzles, from the accursed diamonds that had been our snare, the pasty pig-face of the over-fed pugilist, and the flaming cheeks and hook nose of Rosenthall himself. I was looking beyond them at the doorway filled with quivering silk and plush, black faces, white eyeballs, woolly pates. But a sudden silence recalled my attention to the millionaire. And only his nose retained its color.

"What d'ye mean?" he whispered with a hoarse oath. "Spit it out, or, by Christmas, I'll drill you!"

"Whort price thet brikewater?" drawled Raffles coolly.

"Eh?"

Rosenthall's revolvers were describing widening orbits.

"Whort price thet brikewater—old *I. D. B.?*"

"Where in hell did you get hold o' that?" asked Rosenthall, with a rattle in his thick neck, meant for mirth.

"You may well arst," says Raffles. "It's all over the plice w'ere *I* come from."

"Who can have spread such rot?"

"I dunno," says Raffles; "arst the gen'leman on yer left; p'r'aps *'e* knows."

The gentleman on his left had turned livid with emotion. Guilty conscience never declared itself in plainer terms. For a moment his small eyes bulged like currants in the suet of his face; the next, he had pocketed his pistols on a professional instinct, and was upon us with his fists.

"Out o' the light—out o' the light!" yelled Rosenthall in a frenzy.

He was too late. No sooner had the burly pugilist obstructed his fire than Raffles was through the window at a bound; while I, for standing still and saying nothing, was scientifically felled to the floor.

I cannot have been many moments without my senses. When I recovered them there was a great to-do in the garden, but I had the drawing-room to myself. I sat up. Rosenthall and Purvis were rushing about outside, cursing the Kaffirs and nagging at each other.

"Over *that* wall, I tell yer!"

"I tell you it was this one. Can't you whistle for the police?"

"Police be damned! I've had enough of the blessed police."

"Then we'd better get back and make sure of the other rotter."

"Oh, make sure o' yer skin. That's what you'd better do. Jala, you black hog, if I catch *you* skulkin'. . . ."

I never heard the threat. I was creeping from the drawing-room on my hands and knees, my own revolver swinging by its steel ring from my teeth.

For an instant I thought that the hall also was deserted. I was wrong, and I crept upon a Kaffir on all fours. Poor devil, I could not bring myself to deal him a base blow, but I threatened him most hideously with my revolver, and left the white teeth chattering in his black head as I took the stairs three at a time. Why I went upstairs in that decisive fashion, as though it were my only course, I cannot explain. But garden and ground floor seemed alive with men, and I might have done worse.

I turned into the first room I came to. It was a bedroom—empty, though lit up; and never shall I forget how I started as I entered, on encountering the awful villain that was myself at full length in a pier-glass! Masked, armed, and ragged, I was indeed fit carrion for a bullet or the hangman, and to one or the other I made up my mind. Nevertheless, I hid myself in the wardrobe behind the mirror; and there I stood shivering and cursing my fate, my folly, and Raffles most of all—Raffles first and last—for I daresay half an hour. Then the wardrobe door was flung suddenly open; they had stolen into the room without a sound; and I was hauled downstairs, an ignominious captive.

Gross scenes followed in the hall; the ladies were now upon the stage, and at sight of the desperate criminal they screamed with one accord. In truth I must have given them fair cause, though my mask was now torn away and hid nothing but my left ear. Rosenthall answered their shrieks with a roar for silence; the woman with the bath-sponge hair swore at him shrilly in return; the place became a Babel impossible to describe. I remember wondering how long it would be before the police appeared. Purvis and the ladies were for calling them in and giving me in charge without delay. Rosenthal would not hear of it. He swore that he would shoot man or woman who left his sight. He had had enough of the police. He was not going to have them coming there to spoil sport; he was going to deal with me in his own way. With that he dragged me from all other hands, flung me against a door, and sent a bullet crashing through the wood within an inch of my ear.

"You drunken fool! It'll be murder!" shouted Purvis, getting in the way a second time.

"Wha' do I care? He's armed, isn't he? I shot him in self-defence. It'll be a warning to others. Will you stand aside, or d'ye want it yourself?"

"You're drunk," said Purvis, still between us. "I saw you take a neat tumblerful since you come in, and it's made you drunk as a fool. Pull yourself together, old man. You ain't a-going to do what you'll be sorry for."

"Then I won't shoot at him, I'll only shoot roun' an' roun' the beggar. You're quite right, ole feller. Wouldn't hurt him. Great mishtake. Roun' an' roun'. There—like that!"

His freckled paw shot up over Purvis's shoulder, mauve lightning came from his ring, a red flash from his revolver, and shrieks from the women as the reverberations died away. Some splinters lodged in my hair.

Next instant the prize-fighter disarmed him; and I was safe from the devil, but finally doomed to the deep sea. A policeman was in our midst. He had entered through the drawing-room window; he was an officer of few words and creditable promptitude. In a twinkling he had the handcuffs on my wrists, while the pugilist explained the situation, and his patron reviled the force and its representative with impotent malignity. A fine watch they kept; a lot of good they did; coming in when all was over and the whole household might have been murdered in their sleep. The officer only deigned to notice him as he marched me off.

"We know all about *you*, sir," said he contemptuously, and he refused the sovereign Purvis proffered. "You will be seeing me again, sir, at Marylebone."

"Shall I come now?"

A Costume Piece

"As you please, sir. I rather think the other gentleman requires you more, and I don't fancy this young man means to give much trouble."

"Oh, I'm coming quietly," I said.

And I went.

In silence we traversed perhaps a hundred yards. It must have been midnight. We did not meet a soul. At last I whispered:

"How on earth did you manage it?"

"Purely by luck," said Raffles. "I had the luck to get clear away through knowing every brick of those back-garden walls, and the double luck to have these togs with the rest over at Chelsea. The helmet is one of a collection I made up at Oxford; here it goes over this wall, and we'd better carry the coat and belt before we meet a real officer. I got them once for a fancy ball—ostensibly—and thereby hangs a yarn. I always thought they might come in useful a second time. My chief crux to-night was getting rid of the hansom that brought me back. I sent him off to Scotland Yard with ten bob and a special message to good old Mackenzie. The whole detective department will be at Rosenthall's in about half an hour. Of course, I speculated on our gentleman's hatred of the police—another huge slice of luck. If you'd got away, well and good; if not, I felt he was the man to play with his mouse as long as possible. Yes, Bunny, it's been more of a costume piece than I intended, and we've come out of it with a good deal less credit. But, by Jove, we're jolly lucky to have come out of it at all!"

Gentlemen and Players

OLD Raffles may or may not have been an exceptional criminal, but as a cricketer I dare swear he was unique. Himself a dangerous bat, a brilliant field, and perhaps the very finest slow bowler of his decade, he took incredibly little interest in the game at large. He never went up to Lord's without his cricket-bag, or showed the slightest interest in the result of a match in which he was not himself engaged. Nor was this mere hateful egotism on his part. He professed to have lost all enthusiasm for the game, and to keep it up only from the very lowest motives.

"Cricket," said Raffles, "like everything else, is good enough sport until you discover a better. As a source of excitement it isn't in it with other things you wot of, Bunny, and the involuntary comparison becomes a bore. What's the satisfaction of taking a man's wicket when you want his spoons? Still, if you can bowl a bit your low cunning won't get rusty, and always looking for the weak spot's just the kind of mental exercise one wants. Yes, perhaps there's some affinity between the two things after all. But I'd chuck up cricket to-morrow, Bunny, if it wasn't for the glorious protection it affords a person of my proclivities."

"How so?" said I. "It brings you before the public, I should have thought, far more than is either safe or wise."

"My dear Bunny, that's exactly where you make a mistake. To follow Crime with reasonable impunity you simply *must* have a parallel, ostensible career—the more public the better. The principle is obvious. Mr. Peace, of pious memory, disarmed suspicion by acquiring a local reputation for playing the fiddle and taming animals, and it's my profound conviction that Jack the Ripper was a really eminent public man, whose speeches were very likely reported alongside his atrocities. Fill the bill in some prominent part, and you'll never be suspected of doubling it with another of equal prominence. That's why I want you to cultivate journalism, my boy, and sign all you can. And it's the one and only reason why I don't burn my bats for firewood."

Nevertheless, when he did play there was no keener performer on the field, nor one more anxious to do well for his side. I remember how he went to the nets, before the first match of the season, with his pocket full of sovereigns, which he put on the stumps instead of bails. It was a sight to see the professionals bowling like demons for the hard cash, for whenever a stump was hit a pound was tossed to the bowler and another balanced in its stead, while one man took £3 with a ball that spreadeagled the wicket. Raffles's practice cost him either eight or nine sovereigns; but he had absolutely first-class bowling all the time; and he made fifty-seven runs that day.

It became my pleasure to accompany him to all his matches, to watch every ball he bowled, or played, or fielded, and to sit chatting with him in the pavilion when he was doing none of these three things. You might have seen us there, side by side, during the greater part of the Gentlemen's first innings against the Players (who had lost the toss) on the second Monday in July. We were to be seen, but not heard, for Raffles had failed to score, and was uncommonly cross for a player who cared so little for the game. Merely taciturn with me, he was positively rude to more than one member who wanted to know how it had happened, or who ventured to commiserate him on his luck; there he sat, with a straw hat tilted over his nose and a cigarette stuck between lips that curled disagreeably at every advance. I was therefore much surprised when a young fellow of the exquisite type came and squeezed himself in between us, and met with a perfectly civil reception despite the liberty. I did not know the boy by sight, nor did Raffles introduce us; but their conversation proclaimed at once a slightness of acquaintanceship and a license on the lad's part which combined to puzzle me. Mystification reached its height when Raffles was informed that the other's father was anxious to meet him, and he instantly consented to gratify that whim.

"He's in the Ladies' Enclosure. Will you come round now?"

"With pleasure," says Raffles. "Keep a place for me, Bunny."

And they were gone.

"Young Crowley," said some voice further back. "Last year's Harrow Eleven."

"I remember him. Worst man in the team."

"Keen cricketer, however. Stopped till he was twenty to get his colors. Governor made him. Keen breed. Oh, pretty, sir! Very pretty!"

The game was boring me. I only came to see old Raffles perform. Soon I was looking wistfully for his return, and at length I saw him beckoning me from the palings to the right.

"Want to introduce you to old Amersteth," he whispered, when I joined him. "They've a cricket week next month, when this boy Crowley comes of age, and we've both got to go down and play."

"Both!" I echoed. "But I'm no cricketer!"

"Shut up," says Raffles. "Leave that to me. I've been lying for all I'm worth," he added sepulchrally as we reached the bottom of the steps. "I trust to you not to give the show away."

There was a gleam in his eye that I knew well enough elsewhere, but was unprepared for in those healthy, sane surroundings; and it was with very definite misgivings and surmises that I followed the Zingari blazer through the vast flower-bed of hats and bonnets that bloomed beneath the ladies' awning.

Lord Amersteth was a fine-looking man with a short mustache and a double chin. He received me with much dry courtesy, through which, however, it was not difficult to read a less flattering tale. I was accepted as the inevitable appendage of the invaluable Raffles, with whom I felt deeply incensed as I made my bow.

"I have been bold enough," said Lord Amersteth, "to ask one of the Gentlemen of England to come down and play some rustic cricket for us next month. He is kind enough to say that he would have liked nothing better, but for this little fishing expedition of yours, Mr. ——, Mr. ——," and Lord Amersteth succeeded in remembering my name.

It was, of course, the first I had ever heard of that fishing expedition, but I made haste to say that it could easily, and should certainly, be put off. Raffles gleamed approval through his eyelashes. Lord Amersteth bowed and shrugged.

"You're very good, I'm sure," said he. "But I understand you're a cricketer yourself?"

"He was one at school," said Raffles, with infamous readiness.

"Not a real cricketer," I was stammering meanwhile.

"In the eleven?" said Lord Amersteth.

"I'm afraid not," said I.

"But only just out of it," declared Raffles, to my horror.

"Well, well, we can't all play for the Gentlemen," said Lord Amersteth slyly. "My son Crowley only just scraped into the eleven at Harrow, and *he's* going to play. I may even come in myself at a pinch; so you won't be the only duffer, if you are one, and I shall be very glad if you will come down and help us too. You shall flog a stream before breakfast and after dinner, if you like."

"I should be very proud," I was beginning, as the mere prelude to resolute excuses; but the eye of Raffles opened wide upon me; and I hesitated weakly, to be duly lost.

"Then that's settled," said Lord Amersteth, with the slightest suspicion of grimness. "It's to be a little week, you know, when my son comes of age. We play the Free Foresters, the Dorsetshire Gentlemen, and probably some local lot as well. But Mr. Raffles will tell you all about it, and Crowley shall write. Another wicket! By Jove, they're all out! Then I rely on you both." And, with a little nod, Lord Amersteth rose and sidled to the gangway.

Raffles rose also, but I caught the sleeve of his blazer.

"What are you thinking of?" I whispered savagely. "I was nowhere near the eleven. I'm no sort of cricketer. I shall have to get out of this!"

"Not you," he whispered back. "You needn't play, but come you must. If you wait for me after half-past six I'll tell you why."

But I could guess the reason; and I am ashamed to say that it revolted me much less than did the notion of making a public fool of myself on a cricket-field. My gorge rose at this as it no longer rose at crime, and it was in no tranquil humor that I strolled about the ground while Raffles disappeared in the pavilion. Nor was my annoyance lessened by a little meeting I witnessed between young Crowley and his father, who shrugged as he stopped and stooped to convey some information which made the young man look a little blank. It may have been pure self-consciousness on my part, but I could have sworn that the trouble was their inability to secure the great Raffles without his insignificant friend.

Then the bell rang, and I climbed to the top of the pavilion to watch Raffles bowl. No subleties are lost up there; and if ever a bowler was full of them, it was A. J. Raffles on this day, as, indeed, all the cricket world remembers. One had not to be a cricketer oneself to appreciate his perfect command of pitch and break, his beautifully easy action, which never varied with the varying pace, his great ball on the leg-stump—his dropping head-ball—in a word, the infinite ingenuity of that versatile attack. It was no mere exhibition of athletic prowess, it was an intellectual treat, and one with a special significance in my eyes. I saw the "affinity between the two things," saw it in that afternoon's tireless warfare against the flower of professional cricket. It was not that Raffles took many wickets for few runs; he was too fine a bowler to mind being hit; and time was short, and the wicket good. What I admired, and what I remember, was the combination of resource and cunning, of patience and precision, of head-work and handiwork, which made every over an artistic whole. It was all so characteristic of that other Raffles whom I alone knew!

"I felt like bowling this afternoon," he told me later in the hansom. "With a pitch to help me, I'd have done something big; as it is, three for forty-one, out of the four that fell, isn't so bad for a slow bowler on a plumb wicket against those fellows. But I felt venomous! Nothing riles me more than being asked about for my cricket as though I were a pro. myself."

"Then why on earth go?"

"To punish them, and—because we shall be jolly hard up, Bunny, before the season's over!"

"Ah!" said I. "I thought it was that."

"Of course, it was! It seems they're going to have the very devil of a week of it—balls—dinner parties—swagger house party—general junketings—and obviously a houseful of diamonds as well. Diamonds galore! As a general rule nothing would induce me to abuse my position as a guest. I've never done it, Bunny. But in this case we're engaged like the waiters and the band, and by heaven we'll take our toll! Let's have a quiet dinner somewhere and talk it over."

"It seems rather a vulgar sort of theft," I could not help saying; and to this, my single protest, Raffles instantly assented.

"It *is* a vulgar sort," said he; "but I can't help that. We're getting vulgarly hard up again, and there's an end on 't. Besides, these people deserve it, and can afford it. And don't you run away with the idea that all will be plain sailing; nothing will be easier than getting some stuff, and nothing harder than avoiding all suspicion, as, of course, we must. We may come away with no more than a good working plan of the premises. Who knows? In any case there's weeks of thinking in it for you and me."

But with those weeks I will not weary you further than by remarking that the "thinking," was done entirely by Raffles, who did not always trouble to communicate his thoughts to me. His reticence, however, was no longer an irritant. I began to accept it as a necessary convention of these little enterprises. And, after our last adventure of the kind, more especially after its *dénouement,* my trust in Raffles was much too solid to be shaken by a want of trust in me, which I still believe to have been more the instinct of the criminal than the judgment of the man.

It was on Monday, the tenth of August, that we were due at Milchester Abbey, Dorset; and the beginning of the month found us cruising about that very county, with fly-rods actually in our hands. The idea was that we should acquire at once a local reputation as decent fishermen, and some knowledge of the countryside, with a view to further and more deliberate operations in the event of an unprofitable week. There was another idea which Raffles kept to himself until he had got me down there. Then one day he produced a cricket-ball in a meadow we were crossing, and threw me catches for an hour together. More hours he spent in bowling to me on the nearest green; and, if I was never a cricketer, at least I came nearer to being one, by the end of that week, than ever before or since.

Incident began early on the Monday. We had sallied forth from a desolate little junction within quite a few miles of Milchester, had been caught in a shower, had run for shelter to a wayside inn. A florid, overdressed man was drinking in the parlor, and I could have sworn it was at the sight of him that Raffles recoiled on the threshold, and afterwards insisted on returning to the station through the rain. He assured me, however, that the odor of stale ale had almost knocked him down. And I had to make what I could of his speculative, downcast eyes and knitted brows.

Milchester Abbey is a gray, quadrangular pile, deep-set in rich woody country, and twinkling with triple rows of quaint windows, every one of which seemed alight as we drove up just in time to dress for dinner. The carriage had whirled us under I know not how many triumphal arches in process of construction, and past the tents and flag-poles of a juicy-looking cricket-field, on which Raffles undertook to bowl up to his reputation. But the chief signs of festival were within, where we found an enormous house-party assembled, including more persons of pomp, majesty, and dominion than I had ever encountered in one room before. I confess I felt overpowered. Our errand and my own pretences combined to rob me of an address upon which I have sometimes plumed myself; and I have a grim recollection of my nervous relief when dinner was at last announced. I little knew what an ordeal it was to prove.

I had taken in a much less formidable young lady than might have fallen to my lot. Indeed I began by blessing my good fortune in this respect. Miss Melhuish was merely the rector's daughter, and she had only been asked to make an even number. She informed me of both facts before the soup reached us, and her subsequent conversation was characterized by the same engaging candor. It exposed what was little short of a mania for imparting information. I had simply to listen, to nod, and to be thankful. When I confessed to knowing very few of those present, even by sight, my entertaining companion proceeded to tell me who everybody was, beginning on my left and working conscientiously round to her right. This lasted quite a long time, and really interested me; but a great deal that followed did not, and, obviously to recapture my unworthy attention, Miss Melhuish suddenly asked me, in a sensational whisper, whether I could keep a secret.

I said I thought I might, whereupon another question followed, in still lower and more thrilling accents:

"Are you afraid of burglars?"

Burglars! I was roused at last. The word stabbed me. I repeated it in horrified query.

"So I've found something to interest you at last!" said Miss Melhuish, in naïve triumph. "Yes—burglars! But don't speak so loud. It's supposed to be kept a great secret. I really oughtn't to tell you at all!"

"But what is there to tell?" I whispered with satisfactory impatience.

"You promise not to speak of it?"

"Of course!"

"Well, then, there are burglars in the neighborhood."

"Have they committed any robberies?"

"Not yet."

"Then how do you know?"

"They've been seen. In the district. Two well-known London thieves!"

Two! I looked at Raffles. I had done so often during the evening, envying him his high spirits, his iron nerve, his buoyant wit, his perfect ease and self-possession. But now I pitied him; through all my own terror and consternation, I pitied him as he sat eating and drinking, and laughing and talking, without a cloud of fear or of embarrassment on his handsome, taking, daredevil face. I caught up my champagne and emptied the glass.

"Who has seen them?" I then asked calmly.

"A detective. They were traced down from town a few days ago. They are believed to have designs on the Abbey!"

"But why aren't they run in?"

"Exactly what I asked papa on the way here this evening; he says there is no warrant out against the men at present, and all that can be done is to watch their movements."

"Oh! so they are being watched?"

"Yes, by a detective who is down here on purpose. And I heard Lord Amersteth tell papa that they had been seen this afternoon at Warbeck Junction!"

The very place where Raffles and I had been caught in the rain! Our stampede from the inn was now explained; on the other hand, I was no longer to be taken by surprise by anything that my companion might have to tell me; and I succeeded in looking her in the face with a smile.

"This is really quite exciting, Miss Melhuish," said I. "May I ask how you come to know so much about it?"

"It's papa," was the confidential reply. "Lord Amersteth consulted him, and he consulted me. But for goodness' sake don't let it get about! I can't think *what* tempted me to tell you!"

"You may trust me, Miss Melhuish. But— aren't you frightened?"

Miss Melhuish giggled.

"Not a bit! They won't come to the rectory. There's nothing for them there. But look round the table: look at the diamonds: look at old Lady Melrose's necklace alone!"

The Amateur Cracksman

The Dowager Marchioness of Melrose was one of the few persons whom it had been unnecessary to point out to me. She sat on Lord Amersteth's right, flourishing her ear-trumpet, and drinking champagne with her usual notorious freedom, as dissipated and kindly a dame as the world has ever seen. It was a necklace of diamonds and sapphires that rose and fell about her ample neck.

"They say it's worth five thousand pounds at least," continued my companion. "Lady Margaret told me so this morning (that's Lady Margaret next your Mr. Raffles, you know); and the old dear *will* wear them every night. Think what a haul they would be! No; we don't feel in immediate danger at the rectory."

When the ladies rose, Miss Melhuish bound me to fresh vows of secrecy; and left me, I should think, with some remorse for her indiscretion, but more satisfaction at the importance which it had undoubtedly given her in my eyes. The opinion may smack of vanity, though, in reality, the very springs of conversation reside in that same human, universal itch to thrill the auditor. The peculiarity of Miss Melhuish was that she must be thrilling at all costs. And thrilling she had surely been.

I spare you my feelings of the next two hours.

Gentlemen and Players

I tried hard to get a word with Raffles, but again and again I failed. In the dining-room he and Crowley lit their cigarettes with the same match, and had their heads together all the time. In the drawing-room I had the mortification of hearing him talk interminable nonsense into the ear-trumpet of Lady Melrose, whom he knew in town. Lastly, in the billiard-room, they had a great and lengthy pool, while I sat aloof and chafed more than ever in the company of a very serious Scotchman, who had arrived since dinner, and who would talk of nothing but the recent improvements in instantaneous photography. He had not come to play in the matches (he told me), but to obtain for Lord Amersteth such a series of cricket photographs as had never been taken before; whether as an amateur or a professional photographer I was unable to determine. I remember, however, seeking distraction in little bursts of resolute attention to the conversation of this bore. And so at last the long ordeal ended; glasses were emptied, men said good-night, and I followed Raffles to his room.

"It's all up!" I gasped, as he turned up the gas and I shut the door. "We're being watched. We've been followed down from town. There's a detective here on the spot!"

"How do *you* know?" asked Raffles, turning upon me quite sharply, but without the least dismay. And I told him how I knew.

"Of course," I added, "it was the fellow we saw in the inn this afternoon."

"The detective?" said Raffles. "Do you mean to say you don't know a detective when you see one, Bunny?"

"If that wasn't the fellow, which is?"

Raffles shook his head.

"To think that you've been talking to him for the last hour in the billiard-room and couldn't spot what he was!"

"The Scotch photographer——"

I paused aghast.

"Scotch he is," said Raffles, "and photographer he may be. He is also Inspector Mackenzie of Scotland Yard — the very man I sent the message to that night last April. And you couldn't spot who he was in a whole hour! O Bunny, Bunny, you were never built for crime!"

"But," said I, "if that was Mackenzie, who was the fellow you bolted from at Warbeck?"

"The man he's watching."

"But he's watching us!"

Raffles looked at me with a pitying eye, and

shook his head again before handing me his open cigarette-case.

"I don't know whether smoking's forbidden in one's bedroom, but you'd better take one of these and stand tight, Bunny, because I'm going to say something offensive."

I helped myself with a laugh.

"Say what you like, my dear fellow, if it really isn't you and I that Mackenzie's after."

"Well, then, it isn't, and it couldn't be, and nobody but a born Bunny would suppose for a moment that it was! Do you seriously think he would sit there and knowingly watch his man playing pool under his nose? Well, he might; he's a cool hand, Mackenzie; but I'm not cool enough to win a pool under such conditions. At least I don't think I am; it would be interesting to see. The situation wasn't free from strain as it was, though I knew he wasn't thinking of us. Crowley told me all about it after dinner, you see, and then I'd seen one of the men for myself this afternoon. You thought it was a detective who made me turn tail at that inn. I really don't know why I didn't tell you at the time, but it was just the opposite. That loud, red-faced brute is one of the cleverest thieves in London, and I once had a drink with him and our mutual fence. I was an Eastender from tongue to toe at the moment, but you will understand that I don't run unnecessary risks of recognition by a brute like that."

"He's not alone, I hear."

"By no means; there's at least one other man with him; and it's suggested that there may be an accomplice here in the house."

"Did Lord Crowley tell you so?"

"Crowley and the champagne between them. In confidence, of course, just as your girl told you; but even in confidence he never let on about Mackenzie. He told me there was a detective in the background, but that was all. Putting him up as a guest is evidently their big secret, to be kept from the other guests because it might offend them, but more particularly from the servants whom he's here to watch. That's my reading of the situation, Bunny, and you will agree with me that it's infinitely more interesting than we could have imagined it would prove."

"But infinitely more difficult for us," said I, with a sigh of pusillanimous relief. "Our hands are tied for this week, at all events."

"Not necessarily, my dear Bunny, though I admit that the chances are against us. Yet I'm not so sure of that either. There are all sorts of possibilities in these three-cornered combinations. Set

Gentlemen and Players

A to watch B, and he won't have an eye left for C. That's the obvious theory, but then Mackenzie's a very big A. I should be sorry to have any boodle about me with that man in the house. Yet it would be great to nip in between A and B and score off them both at once! It would be worth a risk, Bunny, to do that; it would be worth risking something merely to take on old hands like B and his men at their own old game! Eh, Bunny? That would be something like a match. Gentlemen and Players at single wicket, by Jove!"

His eyes were brighter than I had known them for many a day. They shone with the perverted enthusiasm which was roused in him only by the contemplation of some new audacity. He kicked off his shoes and began pacing his room with noise-less rapidity; not since the night of the Old Bohemian dinner to Reuben Rosenthall had Raffles exhibited such excitement in my presence; and I was not sorry at the moment to be reminded of the fiasco to which that banquet had been the prelude.

"My dear A. J.," said I in his very own tone, "you're far too fond of the uphill game; you will eventually fall a victim to the sporting spirit and nothing else. Take a lesson from our last escape, and fly lower as you value our skins. Study the house as much as you like, but do—not—go and shove your head into Mackenzie's mouth!"

My wealth of metaphor brought him to a standstill, with his cigarette between his fingers and a grin beneath his shining eyes.

"You're quite right, Bunny. I won't. I really won't. Yet—you saw old Lady Melrose's necklace? I've been wanting it for years! But I'm not going to play the fool; honor bright, I'm not; yet —by Jove!—to get to windward of the professors and Mackenzie too! It would be a great game, Bunny, it would be a great game!"

"Well, you mustn't play it this week."

"No, no, I won't. But I wonder how the professors think of going to work? That's what one wants to know. I wonder if they've really got an accomplice in the house? How I wish I knew their game! But it's all right, Bunny; don't you be jealous; it shall be as you wish."

And with that assurance I went off to my own room, and so to bed with an incredibly light heart. I had still enough of the honest man in me to welcome the postponement of our actual felonies, to dread their performance, to deplore their necessity: which is merely another way of stating the too patent fact that I was an incomparably weaker man than Raffles, while every whit as wicked. I had, however, one rather strong point. I possessed the gift of dismissing unpleasant considerations, not intimately connected with the passing moment, entirely from my mind. Through the exercise of this faculty I had lately been living my frivolous life in town with as much ignoble enjoyment as I had derived from it the year before; and similarly, here at Milchester, in the long-dreaded cricket-week, I had after all a quite excellent time.

It is true that there were other factors in this pleasing disappointment. In the first place, *mirabile dictu,* there were one or two even greater duffers than I on the Abbey cricket-field. Indeed, quite early in the week, when it was of most value to me, I gained considerable kudos for a lucky catch; a ball, of which I had merely heard the hum, stuck fast in my hand, which Lord Amersteth himself grasped in public congratulation. This happy accident was not to be undone even by me, and, as nothing succeeds like success, and the constant encouragement of the one great cricketer on the field was in itself an immense stimulus, I actually made a run or two in my very next innings. Miss Melhuish said pretty things to me that night at the great ball in honor of Viscount Crowley's majority; she also told me that was the night on which the robbers would assuredly make their raid, and was full of arch tremors when we sat out in the garden, though the entire premises were illuminated all night long. Meanwhile the quiet Scotchman took countless photographs by day, which he developed by night in a dark room admirably situated in the servants' part of the house; and it is my firm belief that only two of his fellow-guests knew Mr. Clephane of Dundee for Inspector Mackenzie of Scotland Yard.

The week was to end with a trumpery match on the Saturday, which two or three of us intended abandoning early in order to return to town that night. The match, however, was never played. In the small hours of the Saturday morning a tragedy took place at Milchester Abbey.

Let me tell of the thing as I saw and heard it. My room opened upon the central gallery, and was not even on the same floor as that on which Raffles—and I think all the other men—were quartered. I had been put, in fact, into the dressing-room of one of the grand suites, and my too near neighbors were old Lady Melrose and my host and hostess. Now, by the Friday evening the actual festivities were at an end, and, for the first time that week, I must have been sound asleep since midnight, when all at once I found myself sitting up breathless. A heavy thud had come against my door, and now I heard hard breathing and the dull stamp of muffled feet.

"I've got ye," muttered a voice. "It's no use struggling."

It was the Scotch detective, and a new fear turned me cold. There was no reply, but the hard breathing grew harder still, and the muffled feet beat the floor to a quicker measure. In sudden panic I sprang out of bed and flung open my door. A light burnt low on the landing, and by it I could see Mackenzie swaying and staggering in a silent tussle with some powerful adversary.

"Hold this man!" he cried, as I appeared. "Hold the rascal!"

But I stood like a fool until the pair of them backed into me, when, with a deep breath I flung myself on the fellow, whose face I had seen at last. He was one of the footmen who waited at table; and no sooner had I pinned him than the detective loosed his hold.

"Hang on to him," he cried. "There's more of 'em below."

And he went leaping down the stairs, as other doors opened and Lord Amersteth and his son appeared simultaneously in their pyjamas. At that my man ceased struggling; but I was still holding him when Crowley turned up the gas.

"What the devil's all this?" asked Lord Amersteth, blinking. "Who was that ran downstairs?"

"Mac—Clephane!" said I hastily.

"Aha!" said he, turning to the footman. "So you're the scoundrel, are you? Well done! Well done! Where was he caught?"

I had no idea.

"Here's Lady Melrose's door open," said Crowley. "Lady Melrose! Lady Melrose!"

"You forget she's deaf," said Lord Amersteth. "Ah! that'll be her maid."

An inner door had opened; next instant there was a little shriek, and a white figure gesticulated on the threshold.

"Où donc est l'écrin de Madame la Marquise? La fenêtre est ouverte. Il a disparu!"

"Window open and jewel-case gone, by Jove!" exclaimed Lord Amersteth. "Mais comment est Madame la Marquise? Estelle bien?"

"Oui, milor. Elle dort."

"Sleeps through it all," said my lord. "She's the only one, then!"

"What made Mackenzie—Clephane—bolt?" young Crowley asked me.

"Said there were more of them below."

Gentlemen and Players

"Why the devil couldn't you tell us so before?" he cried, and went leaping downstairs in his turn. He was followed by nearly all the cricketers, who now burst upon the scene in a body, only to desert it for the chase. Raffles was one of them, and I would gladly have been another, had not the footman chosen this moment to hurl me from him, and to make a dash in the direction from which they had come. Lord Amersteth had him in an instant; but the fellow fought desperately, and it took the two of us to drag him downstairs, amid a terrified chorus from half-open doors. Eventually we handed him over to two other footmen who appeared with their nightshirts tucked into their trousers, and my host was good enough to compliment me as he led the way outside.

"I thought I heard a shot," he added. "Didn't you?"

"I thought I heard three."

And out we dashed into the darkness.

I remember how the gravel pricked my feet, how the wet grass numbed them as we made for the sound of voices on an outlying lawn. So dark was the night that we were in the cricketers' midst before we saw the shimmer of their pyjamas; and then Lord Amersteth almost trod on Mackenzie as he lay prostrate in the dew.

"Who's this?" he cried. "What on earth's happened?"

"It's Clephane," said a man who knelt over him. "He's got a bullet in him somewhere."

"Is he alive?"

"Barely."

"Good God! Where's Crowley?"

"Here I am," called a breathless voice. "It's no good, you fellows. There's nothing to show which way they've gone. Here's Raffles; he's chucked it, too." And they ran up panting.

"Well, we've got one of them, at all events," muttered Lord Amersteth. "The next thing is to get this poor fellow indoors. Take his shoulders, somebody. Now his middle. Join hands under him. All together, now; that's the way. Poor fellow! Poor fellow! His name isn't Clephane at all. He's a Scotland Yard detective, down here for these very villains!"

Raffles was the first to express surprise; but he had also been the first to raise the wounded man. Nor had any of them a stronger or more tender hand in the slow procession to the house. In a little we had the senseless man stretched on a sofa in the library. And there, with ice on his wound and brandy in his throat, his eyes opened and his lips moved.

Gentlemen and Players

Lord Amersteth bent down to catch the words. "Yes, yes," said he; "we've got one of them safe and sound. The brute you collared upstairs." Lord Amersteth bent lower. "By Jove! Lowered the jewel-case out of the window, did he? And they've got clean away with it! Well, well! I only hope we'll be able to pull this good fellow through. He's off again."

An hour passed: the sun was rising.

It found a dozen young fellows on the settees in the billiard-room, drinking whiskey and soda-water in their overcoats and pyjamas, and still talking excitedly in one breath. A time-table was being passed from hand to hand: the doctor was still in the library. At last the door opened, and Lord Amersteth put in his head.

"It isn't hopeless," said he, "but it's bad enough. There'll be no cricket to-day."

Another hour, and most of us were on our way to catch the early train; between us we filled a compartment almost to suffocation. And still we talked all together of the night's event; and still I was a little hero in my way, for having kept my hold of the one ruffian who had been taken; and my gratification was subtle and intense. Raffles watched me under lowered lids. Not a word had we had together; not a word did we have until we had left the others at Paddington, and were skimming through the streets in a hansom with noiseless tires and a tinkling bell.

"Well, Bunny," said Raffles, "so the professors have it, eh?"

"Yes," said I. "And I'm jolly glad!"

"That poor Mackenzie has a ball in his chest?"

"That you and I have been on the decent side for once."

He shrugged his shoulders.

"You're hopeless, Bunny, quite hopeless! I take it you wouldn't have refused your share if the boodle had fallen to us? Yet you positively enjoy coming off second best—for the second time running! I confess, however, that the professors' methods were full of interest to me. I, for one, have probably gained as much in experience as I have lost in other things. That lowering the jewel-case out of the window was a very simple and effective expedient; two of them had been waiting below for it for hours."

"How do you know?" I asked.

"I saw them from my own window, which was just above the dear old lady's. I was fretting for that necklace in particular, when I went up to turn in for our last night—and I happened to look out of my window. In point of fact, I wanted to see

I saw them from my own window.

whether the one below was open, and whether there was the slightest chance of working the oracle with my sheet for a rope. Of course I took the precaution of turning my light off first, and it was a lucky thing I did. I saw the pros. right down below, and they never saw me. I saw a little tiny luminous disk just for an instant, and then again for an instant a few minutes later. Of course I knew what it was, for I have my own watch-dial daubed with luminous paint; it makes a lantern of sorts when you can get no better. But these fellows were not using theirs as a lantern. They were under the old lady's window. They were watching the time. The whole thing was arranged with their accomplice inside. Set a thief to catch a thief: in a minute I had guessed what the whole thing proved to be."

"And you did nothing!" I exclaimed.

"On the contrary, I went downstairs and straight into Lady Melrose's room——"

"You did?"

"Without a moment's hesitation. To save her jewels. And I was prepared to yell as much into her ear-trumpet for all the house to hear. But the dear lady is too deaf and too fond of her dinner to wake easily."

"Well?"

The Amateur Cracksman

"She didn't stir."

"And yet you allowed the professors, as you call them, to take her jewels, case and all!"

"All but this," said Raffles, thrusting his fist into my lap. "I would have shown it you before, but really, old fellow, your face all day has been worth a fortune to the firm!"

And he opened his fist, to shut it next instant on the bunch of diamonds and of sapphires that I had last seen encircling the neck of Lady Melrose.

Le Premier Pas

THAT night he told me the story of his earliest crime. Not since the fateful morning of the Ides of March, when he had just mentioned it as an unreported incident of a certain cricket tour, had I succeeded in getting a word out of Raffles on the subject. It was not for want of trying; he would shake his head, and watch his cigarette smoke thoughtfully; a subtle look in his eyes, half cynical, half wistful, as though the decent honest days that were no more had had their merits after all. Raffles would plan a fresh enormity, or glory in the last, with the unmitigated enthusiasm of the artist. It was impossible to imagine one throb or twitter of compunction beneath those frankly egotistic and infectious transports. And yet the ghost of a dead remorse seemed still to visit him with the memory of his first felony, so that I had given the story up long before the night of our return from Milchester. Cricket, however, was in the air, and Raffles's cricket-bag back where he sometimes kept it, in the fender, with the remains of an Orient label still adhering to the leather. My eyes had been on this label for some time, and I suppose his eyes had been on mine, for all at once he asked me if I still burned to hear that yarn.

"It's no use," I replied. "You won't spin it. I must imagine it for myself."

"How can you?"

"Oh, I begin to know your methods."

"You take it I went in with my eyes open, as I do now, eh?"

"I can't imagine your doing otherwise."

"My dear Bunny, it was the most unpremeditated thing I ever did in my life!"

His chair wheeled back into the books as he sprang up with sudden energy. There was quite an indignant glitter in his eyes.

"I can't believe that," said I craftily. "I can't pay you such a poor compliment!"

"Then you must be a fool——"

He broke off, stared hard at me, and in a trice stood smiling in his own despite.

"Or a better knave than I thought you, Bunny, and by Jove it's the knave! Well—I suppose I'm fairly drawn; I give you best, as they say out there. As a matter of fact I've been thinking of the thing myself; last night's racket reminds me of it in one or two respects. I tell you what, though, this is an occasion in any case, and I'm going to celebrate it by breaking the one good rule of my life. I'm going to have a second drink!"

The whiskey tinkled, the syphon fizzed, the ice plopped home; and seated there in his pyjamas, with the inevitable cigarette, Raffles told me the story that I had given up hoping to hear. The windows were wide open; the sounds of Piccadilly floated in at first. Long before he finished, the last wheels had rattled, the last brawler was removed, we alone broke the quiet of the summer night.

". . . No, they do you very well, indeed. You pay for nothing but drinks, so to speak, but I'm afraid mine were of a comprehensive character. I had started in a hole, I ought really to have refused the invitation; then we all went to the Melbourne Cup, and I had the certain winner that didn't win, and that's not the only way you can play the fool in Melbourne. I wasn't the steady old stager I am now, Bunny; my analysis was a confession in itself. But the others didn't know how hard up I was, and I swore they shouldn't. I tried the Jews, but they're extra fly out there. Then I thought of a kinsman of sorts, a second cousin of my father's whom none of us knew anything about, except that he was supposed to be in one or other of the Colonies. If he was a rich man, well and good, I would work him; if not there would be no harm done. I tried to get on his tracks, and, as luck would have it, I succeeded (or thought I had) at the very moment when I happened to have a few days to myself. I was cut over on the hand, just before the big Christmas match, and couldn't have bowled a ball if they had played me.

"The surgeon who fixed me up happened to ask me if I was any relation of Raffles of the National Bank, and the pure luck of it almost took my breath away. A relation who was a high official in one of the banks, who would finance me on my mere name—could anything be better? I made up my mind that this Raffles was the man I wanted, and was awfully sold to find next moment that he wasn't a high official at all. Nor had the doctor so much as met him, but had merely read of him in connection with a small sensation at the suburban branch which my namesake managed; an armed robber had been rather pluckily beaten off, with a bullet in him, by this Raffles; and the sort of thing was so common out there that this was the first I had heard of it! A suburban branch— my financier had faded into some excellent fellow with a billet to lose if he called his soul his own. Still a manager was a manager, and I said I would soon see whether this was the relative I was looking for, if he would be good enough to give me the name of that branch.

"'I'll do more,' says the doctor. 'I'll get you the name of the branch he's been promoted to, for I think I heard they'd moved him up one already.' And the next day he brought me the name of the township of Yea, some fifty miles north of Melbourne; but, with the vagueness which characterized all his information, he was unable to say whether I should find my relative there or not.

"'He's a single man, and his intitials are W. F.,' said the doctor, who was certain enough of the immaterial points. 'He left his old post several days ago, but it appears he's not due at the new one till the New Year. No doubt he'll go before then to take things over and settle in. You might find him up there and you might not. If I were you I should write.'

"'That'll lose two days,' said I, 'and more if he isn't there,' for I'd grown quite keen on this up-country manager, and I felt that if I could get at him while the holidays were still on, a little conviviality might help matters considerably.

" 'Then,' said the doctor, 'I should get a quiet horse and ride. You needn't use that hand.'

" 'Can't I go by train?'

" 'You can and you can't. You would still have to ride. I suppose you're a horseman?'

" 'Yes.'

" 'Then I should certainly ride all the way. It's a delightful road, through Whittlesea and over the Plenty Ranges. It'll give you some idea of the bush, Mr. Raffles, and you'll see the sources of the water supply of this city, sir. You'll see where every drop of it comes from, the pure Yan Yean! I wish I had time to ride with you.'

" 'But where can I get a horse?'

"The doctor thought a moment.

" 'I've a mare of my own that's as fat as butter for want of work,' said he. 'It would be a charity to me to sit on her back for a hundred miles or so, and then I should know you'd have no temptation to use that hand.'

" 'You're far too good!' I protested.

" 'You're A. J. Raffles,' he said.

"And if ever there was a prettier compliment, or a finer instance of even Colonial hospitality, I can only say, Bunny, that I never heard of either."

He sipped his whiskey, threw away the stump of his cigarette, and lit another before continuing.

Le Premier Pas

"Well, I managed to write a line to W. F. with my own hand, which, as you will gather, was not very badly wounded; it was simply this third finger that was split and in splints; and next morning the doctor packed me off on a bovine beast that would have done for an ambulance. Half the team came up to see me start; the rest were rather sick with me for not stopping to see the match out, as if I could help them to win by watching them. They little knew the game I'd got on myself, but still less did I know the game I was going to play.

"It was an interesting ride enough, especially after passing the place called Whittlesea, a real wild township on the lower slope of the ranges, where I recollect having a deadly meal of hot mutton and tea, with the thermometer at three figures in the shade. The first thirty miles or so was a good metal road, too good to go half round the world to ride on, but after Whittlesea it was a mere track over the ranges, a track I often couldn't see and left entirely to the mare. Now it dipped into a gully and ran through a creek, and all the time the local color was inches thick; gum-trees galore and parrots all colors of the rainbow. In one place a whole forest of gums had been ring-barked, and were just as though they had been painted white, without a leaf or a living thing for miles.

And the first living thing I did meet was the sort to give you the creeps; it was a riderless horse coming full tilt through the bush, with the saddle twisted round and the stirrup-irons ringing. Without thinking, I had a shot at heading him with the doctor's mare, and blocked him just enough to allow a man who came galloping after to do the rest.

" 'Thank ye, mister,' growled the man, a huge chap in a red checked shirt, with a beard like W. G. Grace, but the very devil of an expression.

" 'Been an accident?' said I, reining up.

" 'Yes,' said he, scowling as though he defied me to ask any more.

" 'And a nasty one,' I said, 'if that's blood on the saddle!'

"Well, Bunny, I may be a blackguard myself, but I don't think I ever looked at a fellow as that chap looked at me. But I stared him out, and forced him to admit that it was blood on the twisted saddle, and after that he became quite tame. He told me exactly what had happened. A mate of his had been dragged under a branch, and had his nose smashed, but that was all; had sat tight after it till he dropped from loss of blood; another mate was with him back in the bush.

"As I've said already, Bunny, I wasn't the old

stager that I am now—in any respect—and we parted good enough friends. He asked me which way I was going, and, when I told him, he said I should save seven miles, and get a good hour earlier to Yea, by striking off the track and making for a peak that we could see through the trees, and following a creek that I should see from the peak. Don't smile, Bunny! I began by saying I was a child in those days. Of course, the short cut was the long way round; and it was nearly dark when that unlucky mare and I saw the single street of Yea.

"I was looking for the bank when a fellow in a white suit ran down from the veranda.

" 'Mr. Raffles?' said he.

" 'Mr. Raffles,' said I, laughing as I shook his hand.

" 'You're late.'

" 'I was misdirected.'

" 'That all? I'm relieved,' he said. 'Do you know what they are saying? There are some brand-new bushrangers on the road between Whittlesea and this—a second Kelly gang! They'd have caught a Tartar in you, eh?'

" 'They would in you,' I retorted, and my *tu quoque* shut him up and seemed to puzzle him. Yet there was much more sense in it than in his compliment to me, which was absolutely pointless.

" 'I'm afraid you'll find things pretty rough,' he resumed, when he had unstrapped my valise, and handed my reins to his man. 'It's lucky you're a bachelor like myself.'

"I could not quite see the point of this remark either, since, had I been married, I should hardly have sprung my wife upon him in this free-and-easy fashion. I muttered the conventional sort of thing, and then he said I should find it all right when I settled, as though I had come to graze upon him for weeks! 'Well,' thought I, 'these Colonials do take the cake for hospitality!' And, still marvelling, I let him lead me into the private part of the bank.

" 'Dinner will be ready in a quarter of an hour,' said he as we entered. 'I thought you might like a tub first, and you'll find all ready in the room at the end of the passage. Sing out if there's anything you want. Your luggage hasn't turned up yet, by the way, but here's a letter that came this morning.'

" 'Not for me?'

" 'Yes; didn't you expect one?'

" 'I certainly did not!'

" 'Well, here it is.'

"And, as he lit me to my room, I read my own

superscription of the previous day—to W. F. Raffles!

"Bunny, you've had your wind bagged at footer, I daresay; you know what that's like? All I can say is that my moral wind was bagged by that letter as I hope, old chap, I have never yet bagged yours. I couldn't speak. I could only stand with my own letter in my hands until he had the good taste to leave me by myself.

"W. F. Raffles! We had mistaken *each other* for W. F. Raffles—for the new manager who had not yet arrived! Small wonder we had conversed at cross-purposes; the only wonder was that we had not discovered our mutual mistake. How the other man would have laughed! But I—I could not laugh. By Jove, no, it was no laughing matter for me! I saw the whole thing in a flash, without a tremor, but with the direst depression from my own single point of view. Call it callous if you like, Bunny, but remember that I was in much the same hole as you've since been in yourself, and that I had counted on this W. F. Raffles even as you counted on A. J. I thought of the man with the W. G. beard—the riderless horse and the bloody saddle—the deliberate misdirection that had put me off the track and out of the way—and now the missing manager and the report of bushrangers at this end. But I simply don't pretend to have felt any personal pity for a man whom I had never seen; that kind of pity's usually cant; and besides, all mine was needed for myself.

"I was in as big a hole as ever. What the devil was I to do? I doubt if I have sufficiently impressed upon you the absolute necessity of my returning to Melbourne in funds. As a matter of fact it was less the necessity than my own determination which I can truthfully ascribe as absolute.

"Money I would have—but how—but how? Would this stranger be open to persuasion—if I told him the truth? No; that would set us all scouring the country for the rest of the night. Why should I tell him? Suppose I left him to find out his mistake . . . would anything be gained? Bunny, I give you my word that I went in to dinner without a definite intention in my head, or one premeditated lie upon my lips. I might do the decent, natural thing, and explain matters without loss of time; on the other hand, there was no hurry. I had not opened the letter, and could always pretend I had not noticed the initials; meanwhile something might turn up. I could wait a little and see. Tempted I already was, but as yet the temptation was vague, and its very vagueness made me tremble.

Le Premier Pas

" 'Bad news, I'm afraid?' said the manager, when at last I sat down at his table.

" 'A mere annoyance,' I answered—I do assure you—on the spur of the moment and nothing else. But my lie was told; my position was taken; from that moment onward there was no retreat. By implication, without realizing what I was doing, I had already declared myself W. F. Raffles. Therefore, W. F. Raffles I would be, in that bank, for that night. And the devil teach me how to use my lie!

Again he raised his glass to his lips—I had forgotten mine. His cigarette-case caught the gaslight as he handed it to me. I shook my head without taking my eyes from his.

"The devil played up," continued Raffles, with a laugh. "Before I tasted my soup I had decided what to do. I had determined to rob that bank instead of going to bed, and to be back in Melbourne for breakfast if the doctor's mare could do it. I would tell the old fellow that I had missed my way and been bushed for hours, as I easily might have been, and had never got to Yea at all. At Yea, on the other hand, the personation and robbery would ever after be attributed to a member of the gang that had waylaid and murdered the new manager with that very object. You are acquiring some experience in such matters, Bunny. I ask you, was there ever a better get-out? Last night's was something like it, only never such a certainty. And I saw it from the beginning—saw to the end before I had finished my soup!

"To increase my chances, the cashier, who also lived in the bank, was away over the holidays, had actually gone down to Melbourne to see us play; and the man who had taken my horse also waited at table; for he and his wife were the only servants, and they slept in a separate building. You may depend I ascertained this before we had finished dinner. Indeed I was by way of asking too many questions (the most oblique and delicate was that which elicited my host's name, Ewbank), nor was I careful enough to conceal their drift.

" 'Do you know,' said this fellow Ewbank, who was one of the downright sort, 'if it wasn't you, I should say you were in a funk of robbers? Have you lost your nerve?'

" 'I hope not,' said I, turning jolly hot, I can tell you; 'but—well, it is not a pleasant thing to have to put a bullet through a fellow!'

" 'No?' said he, coolly. 'I should enjoy nothing better, myself; besides, yours didn't go through.'

" 'I wish it had!' I was smart enough to cry.

Le Premier Pas

" 'Amen!' said he.

"And I emptied my glass; actually I did not know whether my wounded bank-robber was in prison, dead, or at large!

"But, now that I had had more than enough of it, Ewbank would come back to the subject. He admitted that the staff was small; but as for himself, he had a loaded revolver under his pillow all night, under the counter all day, and he was only waiting for his chance.

" 'Under the counter eh?' I was ass enough to say.

" 'Yes; so had you!'

"He was looking at me in surprise, and something told me that to say 'of course—I had forgotten!' would have been quite fatal, considering what I was supposed to have done. So I looked down my nose and shook my head.

" 'But the papers said you had!' he cried.

" 'Not under the counter," said I.

" 'But it's the regulation!'

"For the moment, Bunny, I felt stumped, though I trust I only looked more superior than before, and I think I justified my look.

" 'The regulation!' I said at length, in the most offensive tone at my command. 'Yes, the regulation would have us all dead men! My dear sir,

do you expect your bank robber to let you reach for
your gun in the place where he knows it's kept? I
had mine in my pocket, and I got my chance by
retreating from the counter with all visible re-
luctance.'

"Ewbank stared at me with open eyes and a
five-barred forehead, then down came his fist on the
table.

" 'By God! That was smart! Still,' he added,
like a man who would not be in the wrong, 'the
papers said the other thing, you know!'

" 'Of course,' I rejoined, 'because they said what
I told them. You wouldn't have had me advertise
the fact that I improved upon the bank's regula-
tions, would you?'

"So that cloud rolled over, and by Jove it was
a cloud with a golden lining. Not silver—real
good Australian gold! For old Ewbank hadn't
quite appreciated me till then; he was a hard nut,
a much older man than myself, and I felt pretty
sure he thought me young for the place, and my
supposed feat a fluke. But I never saw a man
change his mind more openly. He got out his
best brandy, he made me throw away the cigar I
was smoking, and opened a fresh box. He was a
convivial-looking party, with a red moustache, and
a very humorous face (not unlike Tom Emmett's),

and from that moment I laid myself out to attack him on his convivial flank. But he wasn't a Rosenthall, Bunny; he had a treble-seamed, hand-sewn head, and could have drunk me under the table ten times over.

" 'All right,' I thought, 'you may go to bed sober, but you'll sleep like a timber-yard!' And I threw half he gave me through the open window, when he wasn't looking.

"But he was a good chap, Ewbank, and don't you imagine he was at all intemperate. Convivial I called him, and I only wish he had been something more. He did, however, become more and more genial as the evening advanced, and I had not much difficulty in getting him to show me round the bank at what was really an unearthly hour for such a proceeding. It was when he went to fetch the revolver before turning in. I kept him out of his bed another twenty minutes, and I knew every inch of the business premises before I shook hands with Ewbank in my room.

"You won't guess what I did with myself for the next hour. I undressed and went to bed. The incessant strain involved in even the most deliberate impersonation is the most wearing thing I know; then how much more so when the impersonation is impromptu! There's no getting your eye in; the next word may bowl you out; it's batting in a bad light all through. I haven't told you of half the tight places I was in during a conversation that ran into hours and became dangerously intimate towards the end. You can imagine them for yourself, and then picture me spread out on my bed, getting my second wind for the big deed of the night.

"Once more I was in luck, for I had not been lying there long before I heard my dear Ewbank snoring like a harmonium, and the music never ceased for a moment; it was as loud as ever when I crept out and closed my door behind me, as regular as ever when I stopped to listen at his. And I have still to hear the concert that I shall enjoy much more. The good fellow snored me out of the bank, and was still snoring when I again stood and listened under his open window.

"Why did I leave the bank first? To catch and saddle the mare and tether her in a clump of trees close by: to have the means of escape nice and handy before I went to work. I have often wondered at the instinctive wisdom of the precaution; unconsciously I was acting on what has been one of my guiding principles ever since. Pains and patience were required: I had to get my saddle without waking the man, and I was not used to catching horses in a horse-paddock. Then I distrusted the poor mare, and I went back to the stables for a hatful of oats, which I left with her in the clump, hat and all. There was a dog, too, to reckon with (our very worst enemy, Bunny); but I had been 'cute enough to make immense friends with him during the evening; and he wagged his tail, not only when I came downstairs, but when I reappeared at the back-door.

"As the *soi-disant* new manager, I had been able, in the most ordinary course, to pump poor Ewbank about anything and everything connected with the working of the bank, especially in those twenty last invaluable minutes before turning in. And I had made a very natural point of asking him where he kept, and would recommend me to keep, the keys at night. Of course I thought he would take them with him to his room; but no such thing; he had a dodge worth two of that. What it was doesn't much matter, but no outsider would have found those keys in a month of Sundays.

"I, of course, had them in a few seconds, and in a few more I was in the strong-room itself. I forgot to say that the moon had risen and was letting quite a lot of light into the bank. I had, however, brought a bit of candle with me from my room; and in the strong-room, which was down some narrow stairs behind the counter in the banking-chamber, I had no hesitation in lighting it. There was no window down there, and, though I could no longer hear old Ewbank snoring, I had not the slightest reason to anticipate disturbance from that quarter. I did think of locking myself in while I was at work, but, thank goodness, the iron door had no keyhole on the inside.

"Well, there were heaps of gold in the safe, but I only took what I needed and could comfortably carry, not much more than a couple of hundred altogether. Not a note would I touch, and my native caution came out also in the way I divided the sovereigns between all my pockets, and packed them up so that I shouldn't be like the old woman of Banbury Cross. Well, you think me too cautious still, but I was insanely cautious then. And so it was that, just as I was ready to go, whereas I might have been gone ten minutes, there came a violent knocking at the outer door.

"Bunny, it was the outer door of the banking-chamber! My candle must have been seen! And there I stood, with the grease running hot over my fingers, in that brick grave of a strong-room!

"There was only one thing to be done. I must trust to the sound sleeping of Ewbank upstairs, open the door myself, knock the visitor down, or shoot him with the revolver I had been new chum enough to buy before leaving Melbourne, and make a dash for that clump of trees and the doctor's mare. My mind was made up in an instant, and I was at the top of the strong-room stairs, the knocking still continuing, when a second sound drove me back. It was the sound of bare feet coming along a corridor.

"My narrow stair was stone, I tumbled down it with little noise, and had only to push open the iron door, for I had left the keys in the safe. As I did so I heard a handle turn overhead, and thanked my gods that I had shut every single door behind me. You see, old chap, one's caution doesn't always let one in!

" 'Who's that knocking?' said Ewbank up above.

"I could not make out the answer, but it sounded to me like the irrelevant supplication of a spent man. What I did hear, plainly, was the cocking of the bank revolver before the bolts were shot back. Then, a tottering step, a hard, short, shallow breathing, and Ewbank's voice in horror—

" 'My God! Good Lord! What's happened to you? You're bleeding like a pig!'

" 'Not now,' came with a grateful sort of sigh.

" 'But you have been! What's done it?'

" 'Bushrangers.'

" 'Down the road?'

" 'This and Whittlesea—tied to tree—cock shots—left me—bleed to death . . .'

The weak voice failed, and the bare feet bolted. Now was my time—if the poor devil had fainted. But I could not be sure, and there I crouched down below in the dark, at the half-shut iron door, not less spellbound than imprisoned. It was just as well, for Ewbank wasn't gone a minute.

" 'Drink this,' I heard him say, and, when the other spoke again, his voice was stronger.

" 'Now I begin to feel alive . . .'

" 'Don't talk!'

" 'It does me good. You don't know what it was, all those miles alone, one an hour at the outside! I never thought I should come through. You must let me tell you—in case I don't!'

" 'Well, have another sip.'

" 'Thank you . . . I said bushrangers; of course, there are no such things nowadays.'

" 'What were they, then?'

" 'Bank-thieves; the one that had the pot shots was the very brute I drove out of the bank at Coburg, with a bullet in him!' "

"I knew it!"

Le Premier Pas

"Of course you did, Bunny; so did I, down in that strong-room; but old Ewbank didn't, and I thought he was never going to speak again.

" 'You're delirious,' he says at last. 'Who in blazes do you think you are?'

" 'The new manager.'

" 'The new manager's in bed and asleep upstairs.'

" 'When did he arrive?'

" 'This evening.'

" 'Call himself Raffles?'

" 'Yes.'

" 'Well, I'm damned!' whispered the real man. 'I thought it was just revenge, but now I see what it was. My dear sir, the man upstairs is an impostor—if he's upstairs still! He must be one of the gang. He's going to rob the bank—if he hasn't done so already!'

" 'If he hasn't done so already,' muttered Ewbank after him; 'if he's upstairs still! By God, if he is, I'm sorry for him!'

"His tone was quiet enough, but about the nastiest I ever heard. I tell you, Bunny, I was glad I'd brought that revolver. It looked as though it must be mine against his, muzzle to muzzle.

" 'Better have a look down here, first,' said the new manager.

" 'While he gets through his window? No, no, he's not down here.'

" 'It's easy to have a look.'

"Bunny, if you ask me what was the most thrilling moment of my infamous career, I say it was that moment. There I stood at the bottom of those narrow stone stairs, inside the strong-room, with the door a good foot open, and I didn't know whether it would creak or not. The light was coming nearer—and I didn't know! I had to chance it. And it didn't creak a bit; it was far too solid and well-hung; and I couldn't have banged it if I tried, it was too heavy; and it fitted so close that I felt and heard the air squeeze out in my face. Every shred of light went out, except the streak underneath, and it brightened. How I blessed that door!

" 'No, he's not down *there*,' I heard, as though through cotton-wool; then the streak went out too, and in a few seconds I ventured to open once more, and was in time to hear them creeping to my room.

"Well, now there was not a fifth of a second to be lost; but I'm proud to say I came up those stairs on my toes and fingers, and out of that bank (they'd gone and left the door open) just as gingerly as though my time had been my own. I didn't even forget to put on the hat that the doctor's mare was eating her oats out of, as well as she could with a bit, or it alone would have landed me. I didn't even gallop away, but just jogged off quietly in the thick dust at the side of the road (though I own my heart was galloping), and thanked my stars the bank was at that end of the township, in which I really hadn't set foot. The very last thing I heard was the two managers raising Cain and the coachman. And now, Bunny——"

He stood up and stretched himself, with a smile that ended in a yawn. The black windows had faded through every shade of indigo; they now framed their opposite neighbors, stark and livid in the dawn; and the gas seemed turned to nothing in the globes.

"But that's not all?" I cried.

"I'm sorry to say it is," said Raffles apologetically. "The thing should have ended with an exciting chase, I know, but somehow it didn't. I suppose they thought I had got no end of a start; then they had made up their minds that I belonged to the gang, which was not so many miles away; and one of them had got as much as he could carry from that gang as it was. But I wasn't to know all that, and I'm bound to say that there was plenty of excitement left for me. Lord, how I made that

poor brute travel when I got among the trees!
Though we must have made it over fifty miles
from Melbourne, we had done it at a snail's pace;
and those stolen oats had brisked the old girl up
to such a pitch that she fairly bolted when she felt
her nose turned south. By Jove, it was no joke,
in and out among those trees, and under branches
with your face in the mane! I told you about the
forest of dead gums? It looked perfectly ghostly
in the moonlight. And I found it as still as I had
left it—so still that I pulled up there, my first halt,
and lay with my ear to the ground for two or three
minutes. But I heard nothing—not a thing but
the mare's bellow and my own heart. I'm sorry,
Bunny; but if ever you write my memoirs, you
won't have any difficulty in working up that chase.
Play those dead gum-trees for all they're worth,
and let the bullets fly like hail. I'll turn round in
my saddle to see Ewbank coming up hell-to-leather
in his white suit, and I'll duly paint it red. Do it
in the third person, and they won't know how it's
going to end."

"But I don't know myself," I complained.
"Did the mare carry you all the way back to
Melbourne?"

"Every rod, pole or perch! I had her well seen
to at our hotel, and returned her to the doctor in

the evening. He was tremendously tickled to hear
that I had been bushed; next morning he brought
me the paper to show me what I had escaped at
Yea!"

"Without suspecting anything?"

"Ah!" said Raffles, as he put out the gas; "that's
a point on which I've never made up my mind.
The mare and her color was a coincidence—luckily
she was only a bay—and I fancied the condition
of the beast must have told a tale. The doctor's
manner was certainly different. I'm inclined to
think he suspected something, though not the right
thing. I wasn't expecting him, and I fear my
appearance may have increased his suspicions."

I asked him why.

"I used to have rather a heavy moustache," said
Raffles, "but I lost it the day after I lost my
innocence."

Wilful Murder

O F the various robberies in which we were both concerned, it is but the few, I find, that will bear telling at any length. Not that the others contained details which even I would hesitate to recount; it is, rather, the very absence of untoward incident which renders them useless for my present purpose. In point of fact our plans were so craftily laid (by Raffles) that the chances of a hitch were invariably reduced to a minimum before we went to work. We might be disappointed in the market value of our haul; but it was quite the exception for us to find ourselves confronted by unforeseen impediments, or involved in a really dramatic dilemma. There was a sameness even in our spoil; for, of course, only the most precious stones are worth the trouble we took and the risks we ran. In short, our most successful escapades would prove the greatest weariness of all in narrative form; and none more so than the dull affair of the Ardagh emeralds, some eight or nine weeks after the Milchester cricket week. The former, however, had a sequel that I would rather forget than all our burglaries put together.

It was the evening after our return from Ireland, and I was waiting at my rooms for Raffles, who had gone off as usual to dispose of the plunder. Raffles had his own method of conducting this very vital branch of our business, which I was well content to leave entirely in his hands. He drove the bargains, I believe, in a thin but subtle disguise of the flashy-seedy order, and always in the Cockney dialect, of which he had made himself a master. Moreover, he invariably employed the same "fence," who was ostensibly a moneylender in a small (but yet notorious) way, and in reality a rascal as remarkable as Raffles himself. Only lately I also had been to the man, but in my proper person. We had needed capital for the getting of these very emeralds, and I had raised a hundred pounds, on the terms you would expect, from a soft-spoken graybeard with an ingratiating smile, an incessant bow, and the shiftiest old eyes that ever flew from rim to rim of a pair of spectacles. So the original sinews and the final spoils of war came in this case from the self-same source— a circumstance which appealed to us both.

But these same final spoils I was still to see, and

The Amateur Cracksman

I waited and waited with an impatience that grew upon me with the growing dusk. At my open window I had played Sister Ann until the faces in the street below were no longer distinguishable. And now I was tearing to and fro in the grip of horrible hypotheses—a grip that tightened when at last the lift-gates opened with a clatter outside —that held me breathless until a well-known tattoo followed on my door.

"In the dark!" said Raffles, as I dragged him in. "Why, Bunny, what's wrong?"

"Nothing—now you've come," said I, shutting the door behind him in a fever of relief and anxiety. "Well? Well? What did they fetch?"

"Five hundred."

"Down?"

"Got it in my pocket."

"Good man!" I cried. "You don't know what a stew I've been in. I'll switch on the light. I've been thinking of you and nothing else for the last hour. I—I was ass enough to think something had gone wrong!"

Raffles was smiling when the white light filled the room, but for the moment I did not perceive the peculiarity of his smile. I was fatuously full of my own late tremors and present relief; and my first idiotic act was to spill some whiskey and squirt the soda-water all over in my anxiety to do instant justice to the occasion.

"So you thought something had happened?" said Raffles, leaning back in my chair as he lit a cigarette, and looking much amused. "What would you say if something had? Sit tight, my dear chap! It was nothing of the slightest consequence, and it's all over now. A stern chase and a long one, Bunny, but I think I'm well to windward this time."

And suddenly I saw that his collar was limp, his hair matted, his boots thick with dust.

"The police?" I whispered aghast.

"Oh, dear, no; only old Baird."

"Baird! But wasn't it Baird who took the emeralds?"

"It was."

"Then how came he to chase you?"

"My dear fellow, I'll tell you if you give me a chance; it's really nothing to get in the least excited about. Old Baird has at last spotted that I'm not quite the common cracksman I would have him think me. So he's been doing his best to run me to my burrow."

"And you call that nothing!"

"It would be something if he had succeeded;

but he has still to do that. I admit, however, that
he made me sit up for the time being. It all comes
of going on the job so far from home. There was
the old brute with the whole thing in his morning
paper. He *knew* it must have been done by some
fellow who could pass himself off for a gentleman,
and I saw his eyebrows go up the moment I told
him I was the man, with the same old twang that
you could cut with a paper-knife. I did my best to
get out of it—swore I had a pal who was a real
swell—but I saw very plainly that I had given
myself away. He gave up haggling. He paid
my price as though he enjoyed doing it. But I *felt*
him following me when I made tracks; though, of
course, I didn't turn round to see."

"Why not?"

"My dear Bunny, it's the very worst thing you
can do. As long as you look unsuspecting they'll
keep their distance, and so long as they keep their
distance you stand a chance. Once show that you
know you're being followed, and it's flight or fight
for all you're worth. I never even looked round;
and mind you never do in the same hole. I just
hurried up to Blackfriars and booked for High
Street, Kensington, at the top of my voice; and as
the train was leaving Sloane Square out I hopped,
and up all those stairs like a lamplighter, and

round to the studio by the back streets. Well, to be on the safe side, I lay low there all the afternoon, hearing nothing in the least suspicious, and only wishing I had a window to look through instead of that beastly skylight. However, the coast seemed clear enough, and thus far it was my mere idea that he would follow me; there was nothing to show he had. So at last I marched out in my proper rig—almost straight into old Baird's arms!"

"What on earth did you do?"

"Walked past him as though I had never set eyes on him in my life, and didn't then; took a hansom in the King's Road, and drove like the deuce to Clapham Junction; rushed on to the nearest platform, without a ticket, jumped into the first train I saw, got out at Twickenham, walked full tilt back to Richmond, took the District to Charing Cross, and here I am! Ready for a tub and a change, and the best dinner the club can give us. I came to you first, because I thought you might be getting anxious. Come round with me, and I won't keep you long."

"You're certain you've given him the slip?" I said, as we put on our hats.

"Certain enough; but we can make assurance doubly sure," said Raffles, and went to my window,

where he stood for a moment or two looking down
into the street.

"All right?" I asked him.

"All right," said he; and we went downstairs
forthwith, and so to the Albany arm-in-arm.

But we were both rather silent on our way. I, for
my part, was wondering what Raffles would do
about the studio in Chelsea, whither, at all events,
he had been successfully dogged. To me the point
seemed one of immediate importance, but when I
mentioned it he said there was time enough to
think about that. His one other remark was made
after we had nodded (in Bond Street) to a young
blood of our acquaintance who happened to be
getting himself a bad name.

"Poor Jack Rutter!" said Raffles, with a sigh.
"Nothing's sadder than to see a fellow going to
the bad like that. He's about mad with drink and
debt, poor devil! Did you see his eye? Odd that
we should have met him to-night, by the way; it's
old Baird who's said to have skinned him. By
God, but I'd like to skin old Baird!"

And his tone took a sudden low fury, made the
more noticeable by another long silence, which
lasted, indeed, throughout an admirable dinner at
the club, and for some time after we had settled
down in a quiet corner of the smoking-room with

our coffee and cigars. Then at last I saw Raffles looking at me with his lazy smile, and I knew that the morose fit was at an end.

"I daresay you wonder what I've been thinking about all this time?" said he. "I've been thinking what rot it is to go doing things by halves!"

"Well," said I, returning his smile, "that's not a charge that you can bring against yourself, is it?"

"I'm not so sure," said Raffles, blowing a meditative puff; "as a matter of fact, I was thinking less of myself than of that poor devil of a Jack Rutter. There's a fellow who does things by halves; he's only half gone to the bad; and look at the difference between him and us! He's under the thumb of a villainous money-lender; we are solvent citizens. He's taken to drink; we're as sober as we are solvent. His pals are beginning to cut him; our difficulty is to keep the pal from the door. *Enfin,* he begs or borrows, which is stealing by halves; and we steal outright and are done with it. Obviously ours is the more honest course. Yet I'm not sure, Bunny, but we're doing the thing by halves ourselves!"

"Why? What more could we do?" I exclaimed in soft derision, looking round, however, to make sure that we were not overheard.

"What more," said Raffles. "Well, murder—for one thing."

"Rot!"

"A matter of opinion, my dear Bunny; I don't mean it for rot. I've told you before that the biggest man alive is the man who's committed a murder, and not yet been found out; at least he ought to be, but he so very seldom has the soul to appreciate himself. Just think of it! Think of coming in here and talking to the men, very likely about the murder itself; and knowing you've done it; and wondering how they'd look if *they* knew! Oh, it would be great, simply great! But, besides all that, when you were caught there'd be a merciful and dramatic end of you. You'd fill the bill for a few weeks, and then snuff out with a flourish of extra-specials; you wouldn't rust with a vile repose for seven or fourteen years."

"Good old Raffles!" I chuckled. "I begin to forgive you for being in bad form at dinner."

"But I was never more earnest in my life."

"Go on!"

"I mean it."

"You know very well that you wouldn't commit a murder, whatever else you might do."

"I know very well I'm going to commit one to-night!"

Wilful Murder

He had been leaning back in the saddle-bag chair, watching me with keen eyes sheathed by languid lids; now he started forward, and his eyes leapt to mine like cold steel from the scabbard. They struck home to my slow wits; their meaning was no longer in doubt. I, who knew the man, read murder in his clenched hands, and murder in his locked lips, but a hundred murders in those hard blue eyes.

"Baird?" I faltered, moistening my lips with my tongue.

"Of course."

"But you said it didn't matter about the room in Chelsea?"

"I told a lie."

"Anyway you gave him the slip afterwards!"

"That was another. I didn't. I thought I had when I came up to you this evening; but when I looked out of your window—you remember? to make assurance doubly sure—there he was on the opposite pavement down below."

"And you never said a word about it!"

"I wasn't going to spoil your dinner, Bunny, and I wasn't going to let you spoil mine. But there he was as large as life, and, of course, he followed us to the Albany. A fine game for him to play, a game after his mean old heart: blackmail from me, bribes from the police, the one bidding against the other; but he sha'n't play it with me, he sha'n't live to, and the world will have an extortioner the less. Waiter! Two Scotch whiskeys and sodas. I'm off at eleven, Bunny; it's the only thing to be done."

"You know where he lives, then?"

"Yes, out Willesden way, and alone; the fellow's a miser among other things. I long ago found out all about him."

Again I looked round the room; it was a young man's club, and young men were laughing, chatting, smoking, drinking, on every hand. One nodded to me through the smoke. Like a machine I nodded to him, and turned back to Raffles with a groan.

"Surely you will give him a chance!" I urged. "The very sight of your pistol should bring him to terms."

"It wouldn't make him keep them."

"But you might try the effect?"

"I probably shall. Here's a drink for you, Bunny. Wish me luck."

"I'm coming too."

"I don't want you."

"But I must come!"

Wilful Murder

An ugly gleam shot from the steel blue eyes.

"To interfere?" said Raffles.

"Not I."

"You give me your word?"

"I do."

"Bunny, if you break it——"

"You may shoot me, too!"

"I most certainly should," said Raffles, solemnly. "So you come at your own peril, my dear man; but, if you are coming—well, the sooner the better, for I must stop at my rooms on the way."

Five minutes later I was waiting for him at the Piccadilly entrance to the Albany. I had a reason for remaining outside. It was the feeling—half hope, half fear—that Angus Baird might still be on our trail—that some more immediate and less cold-blooded way of dealing with him might result from a sudden encounter between the money-lender and myself. I would not warn him of his danger; but I would avert tragedy at all costs. And when no such encounter had taken place, and Raffles and I were fairly on our way to Willesden, that, I think, was still my honest resolve. I would not break my word if I could help it, but it was a comfort to feel that I could break it if I liked, on an understood penalty. Alas! I fear my good intentions were tainted with a devouring curiosity, and overlaid by the fascination which goes hand in hand with horror.

I have a poignant recollection of the hour it took us to reach the house. We walked across St. James's Park (I can see the lights now, bright on the bridge and blurred in the water), and we had some minutes to wait for the last train to Willesden. It left at 11.21, I remember, and Raffles was put out to find it did not go on to Kensal Rise. We had to get out at Willesden Junction and walk on through the streets into fairly open country that happened to be quite new to me. I could never find the house again. I remember, however, that we were on a dark footpath between woods and fields when the clocks began striking twelve.

"Surely," said I, "we shall find him in bed and asleep?"

"I hope we do," said Raffles grimly.

"Then you mean to break in?"

"What else did you think?"

I had not thought about it at all; the ultimate crime had monopolized my mind. Beside it burglary was a bagatelle, but one to deprecate none the less. I saw obvious objections: the man was *au fait* with cracksmen and their ways: he would certainly have firearms, and might be the first to use them.

Wilful Murder

"I could wish nothing better," said Raffles. "Then it will be man to man, and devil take the worst shot. You don't suppose I prefer foul play to fair, do you? But die he must, by one or the other, or it's a long stretch for you and me."

"Better that than this!"

"Then stay where you are, my good fellow. I told you I didn't want you; and this is the house. So good-night."

I could see no house at all, only the angle of a high wall rising solitary in the night, with the starlight glittering on battlements of broken glass; and in the wall a tall green gate, bristling with spikes, and showing a front for battering-rams in the feeble rays an outlying lamp-post cast across the new-made road. It seemed to me a road of building-sites, with but this one house built, all by itself, at one end; but the night was too dark for more than a mere impression.

Raffles, however, had seen the place by daylight, and had come prepared for the special obstacles; already he was reaching up and putting champagne corks on the spikes, and in another moment he had his folded covert-coat across the corks. I stepped back as he raised himself, and saw a little pyramid of slates snip the sky above the gate; as he squirmed over I ran forward, and had my own weight on the spikes and corks and covert-coat when he gave the latter a tug.

"Coming after all?"

"Rather!"

"Take care, then; the place is all bell-wires and springs. It's no soft thing, this! There—stand still while I take off the corks."

The garden was very small and new, with a grass-plot still in separate sods, but a quantity of full-grown laurels stuck into the raw clay beds. "Bells in themselves," as Raffles whispered; "there's nothing else rustles so—cunning old beast!" And we gave them a wide berth as we crept across the grass.

"He's gone to bed!"

"I don't think so, Bunny. I believe he's seen us."

"Why?"

"I saw a light."

"Where?"

"Downstairs, for an instant, when I——"

His whisper died away; he had seen the light again; and so had I.

It lay like a golden rod under the front-door— and vanished. It reappeared like a gold thread under the lintel—and vanished for good. We heard the stairs creak, creak, and cease, also for good. We neither saw nor heard any more, though we stood waiting on the grass till our feet were soaked with the dew.

"I'm going in," said Raffles at last. "I don't believe he saw us at all. I wish he had. This way."

We trod gingerly on the path, but the gravel stuck to our wet soles, and grated horribly in a little tiled veranda with a glass door leading within. It was through this glass that Raffles had first seen the light; and he now proceeded to take out a pane, with the diamond, the pot of treacle, and the sheet of brown paper which were seldom omitted from his impedimenta. Nor did he dispense with my own assistance, though he may have accepted it as instinctively as it was proffered. In any case it was these fingers that helped to spread the treacle on the brown paper, and pressed the latter to the glass until the diamond had completed its circuit and the pane fell gently back into our hands.

Raffles now inserted his hand, turned the key in the lock, and, by making a long arm, succeeded in drawing the bolt at the bottom of the door; it proved to be the only one, and the door opened, though not very wide.

"What's that?" said Raffles, as something crunched beneath his feet on the very threshold.

The Amateur Cracksman

"A pair of spectacles," I whispered, picking them up. I was still fingering the broken lenses and the bent rims when Raffles tripped and almost fell, with a gasping cry that he made no effort to restrain.

"Hush, man, hush!" I entreated under my breath. "He'll hear you!"

For answer his teeth chattered—even his—and I heard him fumbling with his matches. "No, Bunny; he won't hear us," whispered Raffles, presently; and he rose from his knees and lit a gas as the match burnt down.

Angus Baird was lying on his own floor, dead, with his gray hairs glued together by his blood; near him a poker with the black end glistening; in a corner his desk, ransacked, litttered. A clock ticked noisily on the chimney-piece; for perhaps a hundred seconds there was no other sound.

Raffles stood very still, staring down at the dead, as a man might stare into an abyss after striding blindly to its brink. His breath came audibly through wide nostrils; he made no other sign, and his lips seemed sealed.

"That light!" said I, hoarsely; "the light we saw under the door!"

With a start he turned to me.

Wilful Murder

"It's true! I had forgotten it. It was in here I saw it first!"

"He must be upstairs still!"

"If he is we'll soon rout him out. Come on!"

Instead I laid a hand upon his arm, imploring him to reflect—that his enemy was dead now—that we should certainly be involved—that now or never was our own time to escape. He shook me off in a sudden fury of impatience, a reckless contempt in his eyes, and, bidding me save my own skin if I liked, he once more turned his back upon me, and this time left me half resolved to take him at his word. Had he forgotten on what errand he himself was here? Was he determined that this night should end in black disaster? As I asked myself these questions his match flared in the hall; in another moment the stairs were creaking under his feet, even as they had creaked under those of the murderer; and the humane instinct that inspired him in defiance of his risk was borne in also upon my slower sensibilities. Could we let the murderer go? My answer was to bound up the creaking stairs and to overhaul Raffles on the landing.

But three doors presented themselves; the first opened into a bedroom with the bed turned down but undisturbed; the second room was empty in every sense; the third door was locked.

Raffles lit the landing gas.

"He's in there," said he, cocking his revolver. "Do you remember how we used to break into the studies at school? Here goes!"

His flat foot crashed over the keyhole, the lock gave, the door flew open, and in the sudden draught the landing gas heeled over like a cobble in a squall; as the flame righted itself I saw a fixed bath, two bath-towels knotted together—an open window—a cowering figure—and Raffles struck aghast on the threshold.

"*Jack—Rutter?*"

The words came thick and slow with horror, and in horror I heard myself repeating them, while the cowering figure by the bathroom window rose gradually erect.

"It's you!" he whispered, in amazement no less than our own; "it's you two! What's it mean, Raffles? I saw you get over the gate; a bell rang, the place is full of them. Then you broke in. What's it all mean?"

"We may tell you that, when you tell us what in God's name you've done, Rutter!"

"Done? What have I done?" The unhappy wretch came out into the light with bloodshot, blinking eyes, and a bloody shirt-front. "You know—you've seen—but I'll tell you if you like. I've killed a robber; that's all. I've killed a robber, a usurer, a jackal, a blackmailer, the cleverest and the cruellest villain unhung. I'm ready to hang for him. I'd kill him again!"

And he looked us fiercely in the face, a fine defiance in his dissipated eyes; his breast heaving, his jaw like a rock.

"Shall I tell you how it happened?" he went passionately on. "He's made my life a hell these weeks and months past. You may know that. A perfect hell! Well, to-night I met him in Bond Street. Do you remember when I met you fellows? He wasn't twenty yards behind you; he was on your tracks, Raffles; he saw me nod to you, and stopped me and asked me who you were. He seemed as keen as knives to know, I couldn't think why, and didn't care either, for I saw my chance. I said I'd tell him all about you if he'd give me a private interview. He said he wouldn't. I said he should, and held him by the coat; by the time I let him go you were out of sight, and I waited where I was till he came back in despair. I had the whip-hand of him then. I could dictate where the interview should be, and I made him take me home with him, still swearing to tell him all about you when we'd had our talk. Well, when we got here I made him give me something to eat, putting him off and off; and about ten o'clock I heard the gate shut. I waited a bit, and then asked him if he lived alone.

" 'Not at all,' says he; 'did you not see the servant?'

"I said I'd seen her, but I thought I'd heard her go; if I was mistaken no doubt she would come when she was called; and I yelled three times at the top of my voice. Of course there was no servant to come. I knew that, because I came to see him one night last week, and he interviewed me himself through the gate, but wouldn't open it. Well, when I had done yelling, and not a soul had come near us, he was as white as that ceiling. Then I told him we could have our chat at last; and I picked the poker out of the fender, and told him how he'd robbed me, but, by God, he shouldn't rob me any more. I gave him three minutes to write and sign a settlement of all his iniquitous claims against me, or have his brains beaten out over his own carpet. He thought a minute, and then went to his desk for pen and paper. In two seconds he was round like lightning with a revolver, and I went for him bald-headed. He fired two or three times and missed; you can find the

holes if you like; but I hit him every time—my
God! I was like a savage till the thing was done.
And then I didn't care. I went through his desk
looking for my own bills, and was coming away
when you turned up. I said I didn't care, nor do
I; but I was going to give myself up to-night, and
shall still; so you see I sha'n't give you fellows
much trouble!"

He was done; and there we stood on the landing
of the lonely house, the low, thick, eager voice
still racing and ringing through our ears; the dead
man below, and in front of us his impenitent
slayer. I knew to whom the impenitence would
appeal when he had heard the story, and I was
not mistaken.

"That's all rot," said Raffles, speaking after a
pause; "we sha'n't let you give yourself up."

"You sha'n't stop me! What would be the
good? The woman saw me; it would only be a
question of time; and I can't face waiting to be
taken. Think of it: waiting for them to touch
you on the shoulder! No, no, no; I'll give myself
up and get it over."

His speech was changed; he faltered, floundered.
It was as though a clearer perception of his position had come with the bare idea of escape from it.

"But listen to me," urged Raffles; "We're here

at our peril ourselves. We broke in like thieves
to enforce redress for a grievance very like your
own. But don't you see? We took out a pane—
did the thing like regular burglars. Regular burglars will get the credit of all the rest!"

"You mean that I sha'n't be suspected?"

"I do."

"But I don't want to get off scotfree," cried
Rutter hysterically. "I've killed him. I know
that. But it was in self-defence; it wasn't murder. I must own up and take the consequences.
I shall go mad if I don't!"

His hands twitched; his lips quivered; the tears
were in his eyes. Raffles took him roughly by the
shoulder.

"Look here, you fool! If the three of us were
caught here now, do you know what those consequences would be? We should swing in a row at
Newgate in six weeks' time! You talk as though
we were sitting in a club; don't you know it's one
o'clock in the morning, and the lights on, and a
dead man down below? For God's sake pull
yourself together, and do what I tell you, or you're
a dead man yourself."

"I wish I was one!" Rutter sobbed. "I wish
I had his revolver to blow my own brains out.
It's lying under him. O my God, my God!"

Wilful Murder

His knees knocked together: the frenzy of re-action was at its height. We had to take him downstairs between us, and so through the front door out into the open air.

All was still outside—all but the smothered weeping of the unstrung wretch upon our hands. Raffles returned for a moment to the house; then all was dark as well. The gate opened from within; we closed it carefully behind us; and so left the starlight shining on broken glass and polished spikes, one and all as we had found them.

We escaped; no need to dwell on our escape. Our murderer seemed set upon the scaffold—drunk with his deed, he was more trouble than six men drunk with wine. Again and again we threatened to leave him to his fate, to wash our hands of him. But incredible and unmerited luck was with the three of us. Not a soul did we meet between that and Willesden; and of those who saw us later, did one think of the two young men with crooked white ties, supporting a third in a seemingly unmistakable condition, when the evening papers apprised the town of a terrible tragedy at Kensal Rise?

We walked to Maida Vale, and thence drove openly to my rooms. But I alone went upstairs; the other two proceeded to the Albany, and I saw no more of Raffles for forty-eight hours. He was not at his rooms when I called in the morning; he had left no word. When he reappeared the papers were full of the murder; and the man who had committed it was on the wide Atlantic, a steerage passenger from Liverpool to New York.

"There was no arguing with him," so Raffles told me; "either he must make a clean breast of it or flee the country. So I rigged him up at the studio, and we took the first train to Liverpool. Nothing would induce him to sit tight and enjoy the situation as I should have endeavored to do in his place; and it's just as well! I went to his diggings to destroy some papers, and what do you think I found. The police in possession; there's a warrant out against him already! The idiots think that window wasn't genuine, and the warrant's out. It won't be my fault if it's ever served!"

Nor, after all these years, can I think it will be mine.

Nine Points of the Law

"WELL," said Raffles, "what do you make of it?"

I read the advertisement once more before replying. It was in the last column of the *Daily Telegraph*, and it ran:

TWO THOUSAND POUNDS REWARD—The above sum may be earned by any one qualified to undertake delicate mission and prepared to run certain risk.—Apply by telegram, Security, London.

"I think," said I, "it's the most extraordinary advertisement that ever got into print!"

Raffles smiled.

"Not quite all that, Bunny; still, extraordinary enough, I grant you."

"Look at the figure!"

"It is certainly large."

"And the mission—and the risk!"

"Yes; the combination is frank, to say the least of it. But the really original point is requiring applications by telegram to a telegraphic address! There's something in the fellow who thought of that, and something in his game; with one word

he chokes off the million who answer an advertisement every day—when they can raise the stamp.
My answer cost me five bob; but then I prepaid
another."

"You don't mean to say that you've applied?"

"Rather," said Raffles. "I want two thousand
pounds as much as any man."

"Put your own name?"

"Well—no, Bunny, I didn't. In point of fact
I smell something interesting and illegal, and you
know what a cautious chap I am. I signed myself
Glasspool, care of Hickey, 38, Conduit Street;
that's my tailor, and after sending the wire I went
round and told him what to expect. He promised
to send the reply along the moment it came. I
shouldn't be surprised if that's it!"

And he was gone before a double-knock on the
outer door had done ringing through the rooms,
to return next minute with an open telegram and
a face full of news.

"What do you think?" said he. "Security's
that fellow Addenbrooke, the police-court lawyer,
and he wants to see me *instanter!*"

"Do you know him, then?"

"Merely by repute. I only hope he doesn't
know me. He's the chap who got six weeks for
sailing too close to the wind in the Sutton-Wilmer

case; everybody wondered why he wasn't struck off the rolls. Instead of that he's got a first-rate practice on the seamy side, and every blackguard with half a case takes it straight to Bennett Addenbrooke. He's probably the one man who would have the cheek to put in an advertisement like that, and the one man who could do it without exciting suspicion. It's simply in his line; but you may be sure there's something shady at the bottom of it. The odd thing is that I have long made up my mind to go to Addenbrooke myself if accidents should happen."

"And you're going to him now?"

"This minute," said Raffles, brushing his hat; "and so are you."

"But I came in to drag you out to lunch."

"You shall lunch with me when we've seen this fellow. Come on, Bunny, and we'll choose your name on the way. Mine's Glasspool, and don't you forget it."

Mr. Bennett Addenbrooke occupied substantial offices in Wellington Street, Strand, and was out when we arrived; but he had only just gone "over the way to the court"; and five minutes sufficed to produce a brisk, fresh-colored, resolute-looking man, with a very confident, rather festive air, and black eyes that opened wide at the sight of Raffles.

The Amateur Cracksman

"Mr.—Glasspool?" exclaimed the lawyer.

"My name," said Raffles, with dry effrontery.

"Not up at Lord's, however!" said the other, slyly. "My dear sir, I have seen you take far too many wickets to make any mistake!"

For a single moment Raffles looked venomous; then he shrugged and smiled, and the smile grew into a little cynical chuckle.

"So you have bowled me out in my turn?" said he. "Well, I don't think there's anything to explain. I am harder up than I wished to admit under my own name, that's all, and I want that thousand pounds reward."

"Two thousand," said the solicitor. "And the man who is not above an alias happens to be just the sort of man I want; so don't let that worry you, my dear sir. The matter, however, is of a strictly private and confidential character." And he looked very hard at me.

"Quite so," said Raffles. "But there was something about a risk?"

"A certain risk is involved."

"Then surely three heads will be better than two. I said I wanted that thousand pounds; my friend here wants the other. We are both cursedly hard up, and we go into this thing together or not at all. Must you have his name too? I should give him my real one, Bunny."

Mr. Addenbrooke raised his eyebrows over the card I found for him; then he drummed upon it with his finger-nail, and his embarrassment expressed itself in a puzzled smile.

"The fact is, I find myself in a difficulty," he confessed at last. "Yours is the first reply I have received; people who can afford to send long telegrams don't rush to the advertisements in the *Daily Telegraph;* but, on the other hand, I was not quite prepared to hear from men like yourselves. Candidly, and on consideration, I am not sure that you *are* the stamp of men for me—men who belong to good clubs! I rather intended to appeal to the—er—adventurous classes."

"We are adventurers," said Raffles gravely.

"But you respect the law?"

The black eyes gleamed shrewdly.

"We are not professional rogues, if that's what you mean," said Raffles, smiling. "But on our beam-ends we are; we would do a good deal for a thousand pounds apiece, eh, Bunny?"

"Anything," I murmured.

The solicitor rapped his desk.

"I'll tell you what I want you to do. You can but refuse. It's illegal, but it's illegality in a good cause; that's the risk, and my client is prepared to pay for it. He will pay for the attempt, in case of failure; the money is as good as yours once you consent to run the risk. My client is Sir Bernard Debenham, of Broom Hall, Esher."

"I know his son," I remarked.

Raffles knew him too, but said nothing, and his eye drooped disapproval in my direction. Bennett Addenbrooke turned to me.

"Then," said he, "you have the privilege of knowing one of the most complete young blackguards about town, and the *fons et origo* of the whole trouble. As you know the son, you may know the father too, at all events by reputation; and in that case I needn't tell you that he is a very peculiar man. He lives alone in a storehouse of treasures which no eyes but his ever behold. He is said to have the finest collection of pictures in the south of England, though nobody ever sees them to judge; pictures, fiddles and furniture are his hobby, and he is undoubtedly very eccentric. Nor can one deny that there has been considerable eccentricity in his treatment of his son. For years Sir Bernard paid his debts, and the other day, without the slightest warning, not only refused to do so any more, but absolutely stopped the lad's allowance. Well, I'll tell you what has happened; but first of all you must know, or you may remember, that I appeared for young Debenham in a little scrape he got into a year or two ago. I got him off all right, and Sir Bernard paid me handsomely on the nail. And no more did I hear or see of either of them until one day last week."

The lawyer drew his chair nearer ours, and leant forward with a hand on either knee.

"On Tuesday of last week I had a telegram from Sir Bernard; I was to go to him at once. I found him waiting for me in the drive; without a word he led me to the picture-gallery, which was locked and darkened, drew up a blind, and stood simply pointing to an empty picture-frame. It was a long time before I could get a word out of him. Then at last he told me that that frame had contained one of the rarest and most valuable pictures in England—in the world—an original Velasquez. I have checked this," said the lawyer, "and it seems literally true; the picture was a portrait of the Infanta Maria Teresa, said to be one of the artist's greatest works, second only to another portrait of one of the Popes in Rome—so they told me at the National Gallery, where they had its history by heart. They say there that the picture is practically priceless. And young Debenham has sold it for five thousand pounds!"

The Amateur Cracksman

"The deuce he has," said Raffles.

I inquired who had bought it.

"A Queensland legislator of the name of Craggs
—the Hon. John Montagu Craggs, M.L.C., to
give him his full title. Not that we knew anything
about him on Tuesday last; we didn't even know
for certain that young Debenham had stolen the
picture. But he had gone down for money on the
Monday evening, had been refused, and it was
plain enough that he had helped himself in this
way; he had threatened revenge, and this was it.
Indeed, when I hunted him up in town on the Tuesday night, he confessed as much in the most brazen
manner imaginable. But he wouldn't tell me who
was the purchaser, and finding out took the rest
of the week; but I did find out, and a nice time I've
had of it ever since! Backwards and forwards
between Esher and the Métropole, where the
Queenslander is staying, sometimes twice a day;
threats, offers, prayers, entreaties, not one of them
a bit of good!"

"But," said Raffles, "surely it's a clear case?
The sale was illegal; you can pay him back his
money and force him to give the picture up."

"Exactly; but not without an action and a public scandal, and that my client declines to face.
He would rather lose even his picture than have

the whole thing get into the papers; he has disowned his son, but he will not disgrace him; yet his picture he must have by hook or crook, and there's the rub! I am to get it back by fair means or foul. He gives me *carte blanche* in the matter, and, I verily believe, would throw in a blank check if asked. He offered one to the Queenslander, but Craggs simply tore it in two; the one old boy is as much a character as the other, and between the two of them I'm at my wits' end."

"So you put that advertisement in the paper?" said Raffles, in the dry tones he had adopted throughout the interview.

"As a last resort. I did."

"And you wish us to *steal* this picture?"

It was magnificently said; the lawyer flushed from his hair to his collar.

"I knew you were not the men!" he groaned. "I never thought of men of your stamp! But it's *not* stealing," he exclaimed heatedly; "it's recovering stolen property. Besides, Sir Bernard will pay him his five thousand as soon as he has the picture; and, you'll see, old Craggs will be just as loath to let it come out as Sir Bernard himself. No, no—it's an enterprise, an adventure, if you like—but not stealing."

"You yourself mentioned the law," murmured Raffles.

"And the risk," I added.

"We pay for that," he said once more.

"But not enough," said Raffles, shaking his head. "My good sir, consider what it means to us. You spoke of those clubs; we should not only get kicked out of them, but put in prison like common burglars! It's true we're hard up, but it simply isn't worth it at the price. Double your stakes, and I for one am your man."

Addenbrooke wavered.

"Do you think you could bring it off?"

"We could try."

"But you have no——"

"Experience? Well, hardly!"

"And you would really run the risk for four thousand pounds?"

Raffles looked at me. I nodded.

"We would," said he, "and blow the odds!"

"It's more than I can ask my client to pay," said Addenbrooke, growing firm.

"Then it's more than you can expect us to risk."

"You are in earnest?"

"God wot!"

"Say three thousand if you succeed!"

"Four is our figure, Mr. Addenbrooke."

Nine Points of the Law

"Then I think it should be nothing if you fail."

"Doubles or quits?" cried Raffles. "Well, that's sporting. Done!"

Addenbrooke opened his lips, half rose, then sat back in his chair, and looked long and shrewdly at Raffles—never once at me.

"I know your bowling," said he reflectively. "I go up to Lord's whenever I want an hour's real rest, and I've seen you bowl again and again—yes, and take the best wickets in England on a plumb pitch. I don't forget the last Gentleman and Players; I was there. You're up to every trick—every one . . . I'm inclined to think that if anybody could bowl out this old Australian . . . Damme, I believe you're my very man!"

The bargain was clinched at the Café Royal, where Bennett Addenbrooke insisted on playing host at an extravagant luncheon. I remember that he took his whack of champagne with the nervous freedom of a man at high pressure, and have no doubt I kept him in countenance by an equal indulgence; but Raffles, ever an exemplar in such matters, was more abstemious even than his wont, and very poor company to boot. I can see him now, his eyes in his plate—thinking— thinking. I can see the solicitor glancing from him to me in an apprehension of which I did my best to disabuse him by reassuring looks. At the close Raffles apologized for his preoccupation, called for an A.B.C. time-table, and announced his intention of catching the 3.2 to Esher.

"You must excuse me, Mr. Addenbrooke," said he, "but I have my own idea, and for the moment I should much prefer to keep it to myself. It may end in fizzle, so I would rather not speak about it to either of you just yet. But speak to Sir Bernard I must, so will you write me one line to him on your card? Of course, if you wish, you must come down with me and hear what I say; but I really don't see much point in it."

And as usual Raffles had his way, though Bennett Addenbrooke showed some temper when he was gone, and I myself shared his annoyance to no small extent. I could only tell him that it was in the nature of Raffles to be self-willed and secretive, but that no man of my acquaintance had half his audacity and determination; that I for my part would trust him through and through, and let him gang his own gait every time. More I dared not say, even to remove those chill misgivings with which I knew that the lawyer went his way.

That day I saw no more of Raffles, but a telegram reached me when I was dressing for dinner:

Raffles announced his intention of catching the 3.2 to Esher.

Nine Points of the Law

"Be in your rooms to-morrow from noon and keep rest of day clear, Raffles."

It had been sent off from Waterloo at 6.42.

So Raffles was back in town; at an earlier stage of our relations I should have hunted him up then and there, but now I knew better. His telegram meant that he had no desire for my society that night or the following forenoon; that when he wanted me I should see him soon enough.

And see him I did, towards one o'clock next day. I was watching for him from my window in Mount Street, when he drove up furiously in a hansom, and jumped out without a word to the man. I met him next minute at the lift gates, and he fairly pushed me back into my rooms.

"Five minutes, Bunny!" he cried. "Not a moment more."

And he tore off his coat before flinging himself into the nearest chair.

"I'm fairly on the rush," he panted; "having the very devil of a time! Not a word till I tell you all I've done. I settled my plan of campaign yesterday at lunch. The first thing was to get in with this man Craggs; you can't break into a place like the Métropole, it's got to be done from the inside. Problem one, how to get at the fellow.

161

The Amateur Cracksman

Only one sort of pretext would do—it must be something to do with this blessed picture, so that I might see where he'd got it and all that. Well, I couldn't go and ask to see it out of curiosity, and I couldn't go as a second representative of the other old chap, and it was thinking how I could go that made me such a bear at lunch. But I saw my way before we got up. If I could only lay hold of a copy of the picture I might ask leave to go and compare it with the original. So down I went to Esher to find out if there was a copy in existence, and was at Broom Hall for one hour and a half yesterday afternoon. There was no copy there, but they must exist, for Sir Bernard himself (there's 'copy' *there!*) has allowed a couple to be made since the picture has been in his possession. He hunted up the painters' addresses, and the rest of the evening I spent in hunting up the painters themselves; but their work had been done on commission; one copy had gone out of the country, and I'm still on the track of the other."

"Then you haven't seen Craggs yet?"

"Seen him and made friends with him, and if possible he's the funnier old cuss of the two; but you should study 'em both. I took the bull by the horns this morning, went in and lied like Ananias, and it was just as well I did—the old ruffian sails for Australia by to-morrow's boat. I told him a man wanted to sell me a copy of the celebrated Infanta Maria Teresa of Velasquez, that I'd been down to the supposed owner of the picture, only to find that he had just sold it to him. You should have seen his face when I told him that! He grinned all round his wicked old head. 'Did *old* Debenham admit the sale?' says he; and when I said he had he chuckled to himself for about five minutes. He was so pleased that he did just what I hoped he would do; he showed me the great picture—luckily it isn't by any means a large one—also the case he's got it in. It's an iron map-case in which he brought over the plans of his land in Brisbane; he wants to know who would suspect it of containing an Old Master, too? But he's had it fitted with a new Chubb's lock, and I managed to take an interest in the key while he was gloating over the canvas. I had the wax in the palm of my hand, and I shall make my duplicate this afternoon."

Raffles looked at his watch and jumped up saying he had given me a minute too much.

"By the way," he added, "you've got to dine with him at the Métropole to-night!"

"I?"

"Yes; don't look so scared. Both of us are invited—I swore you were dining with me. I accepted for us both; but I sha'n't be there."

His clear eye was upon me, bright with meaning and with mischief. I implored him to tell me what his meaning was.

"You will dine in his private sitting-room," said Raffles; "it adjoins his bedroom. You must keep him sitting as long as possible, Bunny, and talking all the time!"

In a flash I saw his plan.

"You're going for the picture while we're at dinner?"

"I am."

"If he hears you?"

"He sha'n't."

"But if he does!"

And I fairly trembled at the thought.

"If he does," said Raffles, "there will be a collision, that's all. Revolver would be out of place in the Métropole, but I shall certainly take a life-preserver."

"But it's ghastly!" I cried. "To sit and talk to an utter stranger and to know that you're at work in the next room!"

"Two thousand apiece," said Raffles, quietly.

"Upon my soul I believe I shall give it away!"

Nine Points of the Law

"Not you, Bunny. I know you better than you know yourself."

He put on his coat and his hat.

"What time have I to be there?" I asked him, with a groan.

"Quarter to eight. There will be a telegram from me saying I can't turn up. He's a terror to talk, you'll have no difficulty in keeping the ball rolling; but head him off his picture for all you're worth. If he offers to show it to you, say you must go. He locked up the case elaborately this afternoon, and there's no earthly reason why he should unlock it again in this hemisphere."

"Where shall I find you when I get away?"

"I shall be down at Esher. I hope to catch the 9.55."

"But surely I can see you again this afternoon?" I cried in a ferment, for his hand was on the door. "I'm not half coached up yet! I know I shall make a mess of it!"

"Not you," he said again, "but *I* shall if I waste any more time. I've got a deuce of a lot of rushing about to do yet. You won't find me at my rooms. Why not come down to Esher yourself by the last train? That's it—down you come with the latest news! I'll tell old Debenham to expect you: he shall give us both a bed. By Jove! he won't be able to do us too well if he's got his picture."

"If!" I groaned as he nodded his adieu; and he left me limp with apprehension, sick with fear, in a perfectly pitiable condition of pure stage-fright.

For, after all, I had only to act my part; unless Raffles failed where he never did fail, unless Raffles the neat and noiseless was for once clumsy and inept, all I had to do was indeed to "smile and smile and be a villain." I practised that smile half the afternoon. I rehearsed putative parts in hypothetical conversations. I got up stories. I dipped in a book on Queensland at the club. And at last it was 7.45, and I was making my bow to a somewhat elderly man with a small bald head and a retreating brow.

"So you're Mr. Raffles's friend?" said he, overhauling me rather rudely with his light small eyes. "Seen anything of him? Expected him early to show me something, but he's never come."

No more, evidently, had his telegram, and my troubles were beginning early. I said I had not seen Raffles since one o'clock, telling the truth with unction while I could; even as we spoke there came a knock at the door; it was the telegram at last, and, after reading it himself, the Queenslander handed it to me.

Nine Points of the Law

"Called out of town!" he grumbled. "Sudden illness of near relative! What near relatives has he got?"

I knew of none, and for an instant I quailed before the perils of invention; then I replied that I had never met any of his people, and again felt fortified by my veracity.

"Thought you were bosom pals?" said he, with (as I imagined) a gleam of suspicion in his crafty little eyes.

"Only in town," said I. "I've never been to his place."

"Well," he growled, "I suppose it can't be helped. Don't know why he couldn't come and have his dinner first. Like to see the deathbed *I'd* go to without *my* dinner; it's a full-skin billet, if you ask me. Well, must just dine without him, and he'll have to buy his pig in a poke after all. Mind touching that bell? Suppose you know what he came to see me about? Sorry I sha'n't see him again, for his own sake. I liked Raffles—took to him amazingly. He's a cynic. Like cynics. One myself. Rank bad form of his mother or his aunt, and I hope she will go and kick the bucket."

I connect these specimens of his conversation, though they were doubtless detached at the time, and interspersed with remarks of mine here and there. They filled the interval until dinner was served, and they gave me an impression of the man which his every subsequent utterance confirmed. It was an impression which did away with all remorse for my treacherous presence at his table. He was that terrible type, the Silly Cynic, his aim a caustic commentary on all things and all men, his achievement mere vulgar irreverence and unintelligent scorn. Ill-bred and ill-informed, he had (on his own showing) fluked into fortune on a rise in land; yet cunning he possessed, as well as malice, and he chuckled till he choked over the misfortunes of less astute speculators in the same boom. Even now I cannot feel much compunction for my behavior by the Hon. J. M. Craggs, M.L.C.

But never shall I forget the private agonies of the situation, the listening to my host with one ear and for Raffles with the other! Once I heard him —though the rooms were not divided by the old-fashioned folding-doors, and though the door that did divide them was not only shut but richly curtained, I could have sworn I heard him once. I spilt my wine and laughed at the top of my voice at some coarse sally of my host's. And I heard nothing more, though my ears were on the strain.

Nine Points of the Law

But later, to my horror, when the waiter had finally withdrawn, Craggs himself sprang up and rushed to his bedroom without a word. I sat like stone till he returned.

"Thought I heard a door go," he said. "Must have been mistaken . . . imagination . . . gave me quite a turn. Raffles tell you priceless treasure I got in there?"

It was the picture at last; up to this point I had kept him to Queensland and the making of his pile. I tried to get him back there now, but in vain. He was reminded of his great ill-gotten possession. I said that Raffles had just mentioned it, and that set him off. With the confidential garrulity of a man who has dined too well, he plunged into his darling topic, and I looked past him at the clock. It was only a quarter to ten.

In common decency I could not go yet. So there I sat (we were still at port) and learnt what had originally fired my host's ambition to possess what he was pleased to call a "real, genuine, twin-screw, double-funnelled, copper-bottomed Old Master"; it was to "go one better" than some rival legislator of pictorial proclivities. But even an epitome of his monologue would be so much weariness; suffice it that it ended inevitably in the invitation I had dreaded all the evening.

"But you must see it. Next room. This way."

"Isn't it packed up?" I inquired hastily.

"Lock and key. That's all."

"Pray don't trouble," I urged.

"Trouble be hanged!" said he. "Come along."

And all at once I saw that to resist him further would be to heap suspicion upon myself against the moment of impending discovery. I therefore followed him into his bedroom without further protest, and suffered him first to show me the iron map-case which stood in one corner; he took a crafty pride in this receptacle, and I thought he would never cease descanting on its innocent appearance and its Chubb's lock. It seemed an interminable age before the key was in the latter. Then the ward clicked, and my pulse stood still.

"By Jove!" I cried next instant.

The canvas was in its place among the maps!

"Thought it would knock you," said Craggs, drawing it out and unrolling it for my benefit. "Grand thing, ain't it? Wouldn't think it had been painted two hundred and thirty years? It has, though, *my* word! Old Johnson's face will be a treat when he sees it; won't go bragging about *his* pictures much more. Why, this one's worth all the pictures in Colony o' Queensland put

together. Worth fifty thousand pounds, my boy
—and I got it for five!"

He dug me in the ribs, and seemed in the mood
for further confidences. My appearance checked
him, and he rubbed his hands.

"If you take it like that," he chuckled, "how will
old Johnson take it? Go out and hang himself to
his own picture-rods, I hope!"

Heaven knows what I contrived to say at last.
Struck speechless first by my relief, I continued
silent from a very different cause. A new tangle
of emotions tied my tongue. Raffles had failed—
Raffles had failed! Could I not succeed? Was
it too late? Was there no way?

"So long," he said, taking a last look at the canvas before he rolled it up—"so long till we get to
Brisbane."

The flutter I was in as he closed the case!

"For the last time," he went on, as his keys
jingled back into his pocket. "It goes straight into
the strong-room on board."

For the last time! If I could but send him out
to Australia with only its legitimate contents in
his precious map-case! If I could but succeed
where Raffles had failed!

We returned to the other room. I have no
notion how long he talked, or what about. Whis-

key and soda-water became the order of the hour. I scarcely touched it, but he drank copiously, and before eleven I left him incoherent. And the last train for Esher was the 11.50 out of Waterloo.

I took a hansom to my rooms. I was back at the hotel in thirteen minutes. I walked upstairs. The corridor was empty; I stood an instant on the sitting-room threshold, heard a snore within, and admitted myself softly with my gentleman's own key, which it had been a very simple matter to take away with me.

Craggs never moved; he was stretched on the sofa fast asleep. But not fast enough for me. I saturated my handkerchief with the chloroform I had brought, and laid it gently over his mouth. Two or three stertorous breaths, and the man was a log.

I removed the handkerchief; I extracted the keys from his pocket. In less than five minutes I put them back, after winding the picture about my body beneath my Inverness cape. I took some whiskey and soda-water before I went.

The train was easily caught—so easily that I trembled for ten minutes in my first-class smoking carriage—in terror of every footstep on the platform, in unreasonable terror till the end. Then at last I sat back and lit a cigarette, and the lights of Waterloo reeled out behind.

Some men were returning from the theatre. I can recall their conversation even now. They were disappointed with the piece they had seen. It was one of the later Savoy operas, and they spoke wistfully of the days of "Pinafore" and "Patience." One of them hummed a stave, and there was an argument as to whether the air was out of "Patience" or the "Mikado." They all got out at Surbiton, and I was alone with my triumph for a few intoxicating minutes. To think that I had succeeded where Raffles had failed! Of all our adventures this was the first in which I had played a commanding part; and, of them all, this was infinitely the least discreditable. It left me without a conscientious qualm; I had but robbed a robber, when all was said. And I had done it myself, single-handed—*ipse egomet!*

I pictured Raffles, his surprise, his delight. He would think a little more of me in future. And that future, it should be different. We had two thousand pounds apiece—surely enough to start afresh as honest men—and all through me!

In a glow I sprang out at Esher, and took the one belated cab that was waiting under the bridge. In a perfect fever I beheld Broom Hall, with the lower story still lit up, and saw the front door open as I climbed the steps.

"Thought it was you," said Raffles cheerily. "It's all right. There's a bed for you. Sir Bernard's sitting up to shake your hand."

His good spirits disappointed me. But I knew the man: he was one of those who wear their brightest smile in the blackest hour. I knew him too well by this time to be deceived.

"I've got it!" I cried in his ear. "I've got it!"

"Got what?" he asked me, stepping back.

"The picture!"

"*What?*"

"The picture. He showed it me. You had to go without it; I saw that. So I determined to have it. And here it is."

"Let's see," said Raffles grimly.

I threw off my cape and unwound the canvas from about my body. While I was doing so an untidy old gentleman made his appearance in the hall, and stood looking on with raised eyebrows.

"Looks pretty fresh for an Old Master, doesn't she?" said Raffles.

His tone was strange. I could only suppose that he was jealous of my success.

"So Craggs said. I hardly looked at it myself."

Nine Points of the Law

"Well, look now—look closely. By Jove, I must have faked her better than I thought!"

"It's a copy!" I cried.

"It's *the* copy," he answered. "It's the copy I've been tearing all over the country to procure. It's the copy I faked back and front, so that, on your own showing, it imposed upon Craggs, and might have made him happy for life. And you go and rob him of that!"

I could not speak.

"How did you manage it?" inquired Sir Bernard Debenham.

"Have you killed him?" asked Raffles sardonically.

I did not look at him; I turned to Sir Bernard Debenham, and to him I told my story, hoarsely, excitedly, for it was all that I could do to keep from breaking down. But as I spoke I became calmer, and I finished in mere bitterness, with the remark that another time Raffles might tell me what he meant to do.

"Another time!" he cried instantly. "My dear Bunny, you speak as though we were going to turn burglars for a living!"

"I trust you won't," said Sir Bernard, smiling, "for you are certainly two very daring young men. Let us hope our friend from Queensland will do as he said, and not open his map-case till he gets back there. He will find my check awaiting him, and I shall be very much surprised if he troubles any of us again."

Raffles and I did not speak till I was in the room which had been prepared for me. Nor was I anxious to do so then. But he followed me and took my hand.

"Bunny," said he, "don't you be hard on a fellow! I was in the deuce of a hurry, and didn't know that I should ever get what I wanted in time, and that's a fact. But it serves me right that you should have gone and undone one of the best things I ever did. As for *your* handiwork, old chap, you won't mind my saying that I didn't think you had it in you. In future——"

"Don't talk to me about the future!" I cried. "I hate the whole thing! I'm going to chuck it up!"

"So am I," said Raffles, "when I've made my pile."

The Return Match

I HAD turned into Piccadilly, one thick evening in the following November, when my guilty heart stood still at the sudden grip of a hand upon my arm. I thought—I was always thinking—that my inevitable hour was come at last. It was only Raffles, however, who stood smiling at me through the fog.

"Well met!" said he. "I've been looking for you at the club."

"I was just on my way there," I returned, with an attempt to hide my tremors. It was an ineffectual attempt, as I saw from his broader smile, and by the indulgent shake of his head.

"Come up to my place instead," said he. "I've something amusing to tell you."

I made excuses, for his tone foretold the kind of amusement, and it was a kind against which I had successfully set my face for months. I have stated before, however, and I can but reiterate, that to me, at all events, there was never anybody in the world so irresistible as Raffles when his mind was

177

made up. That we had both been independent of crime since our little service to Sir Bernard Debenham—that there had been no occasion for that masterful mind to be made up in any such direction for many a day—was the undeniable basis of a longer spell of honesty than I had hitherto enjoyed during the term of our mutual intimacy. Be sure I would deny it if I could; the very thing I am to tell you would discredit such a boast. I made my excuses, as I have said. But his arm slid through mine, with his little laugh of light-hearted mastery. And even while I argued we were on his staircase in the Albany.

His fire had fallen low. He poked and replenished it after lighting the gas. As for me, I stood by sullenly in my overcoat until he dragged it off my back.

"What a chap you are!" said Raffles, playfully. "One would really think I had proposed to crack another crib this blessed night! Well, it isn't that, Bunny; so get into that chair, and take one of these Sullivans and sit tight."

He held the match to my cigarette; he brought me a whiskey and soda. Then he went out into the lobby, and, just as I was beginning to feel happy, I heard a bolt shot home. It cost me an effort to remain in that chair; next moment he was straddling another and gloating over my discomfiture across his folded arms.

"You remember Milchester, Bunny, old boy?"

His tone was as bland as mine was grim when I answered that I did.

"We had a little match there that wasn't down on the card. Gentlemen and Players, if you recollect?"

"I don't forget it."

"Seeing that you never got an innings, so to speak, I thought you might. Well, the Gentlemen scored pretty freely, but the Players were all caught."

"Poor devils!"

"Don't be too sure. You remember the fellow we saw in the inn? The florid, over-dressed chap who I told you was one of the cleverest thieves in town?"

"I remember him. Crawshay his name turned out to be."

"Well, it was certainly the name he was convicted under, so Crawshay let it be. You needn't waste any pity on *him,* old chap; he escaped from Dartmoor yesterday afternoon."

"Well done!"

Raffles smiled, but his eyebrows had gone up, and his shoulders followed suit.

The Amateur Cracksman

"You are perfectly right; it was very well done indeed. I wonder you didn't see it in the paper. In a dense fog on the moor yesterday good old Crawshay made a bolt for it, and got away with‧ out a scratch under heavy fire. All honor to him, I agree; a fellow with that much grit deserves his liberty. But Crawshay has a good deal more. They hunted him all night long; couldn't find him for nuts; and that was all you missed in the morn‐ ing papers."

He unfolded a *Pall Mall*, which he had brought in with him.

"But listen to this; here's an account of the escape, with just the addition which puts the thing on a higher level. 'The fugitive has been traced to Totnes, where he appears to have committed a peculiarly daring outrage in the early hours of this morning. He is reported to have entered the lodg‐ ings of the Rev. A. H. Ellingworth, curate of the parish, who missed his clothes on rising at the usual hour; later in the morning those of the convict were discovered neatly folded at the bottom of a drawer. Meanwhile Crawshay had made good his second escape, though it is believed that so distinctive a guise will lead to his recapture during the day.' What do you think of that, Bunny?"

The Return Match

"He is certainly a sportsman," said I, reaching for the paper.

"He's more," said Raffles, "he's an artist, and I envy him. The curate, of all men! Beautiful—beautiful! But that's not all. I saw just now on the board at the club that there's been an outrage on the line near Dawlish. Parson found insensible in the six-foot way. Our friend again! The telegram doesn't say so, but it's obvious; he's simply knocked some other fellow out, changed clothes again, and come on gayly to town. Isn't it great? I do believe it's the best thing of the kind that's ever been done!"

"But why should he come to town?"

In an instant the enthusiasm faded from Raffles's face; clearly I had reminded him of some prime anxiety, forgotten in his impersonal joy over the exploit of a fellow-criminal. He looked over his shoulder towards the lobby before replying.

"I believe," said he, "that the beggar's on *my* tracks!"

And as he spoke he was himself again—quietly amused—cynically unperturbed—characteristically enjoying the situation and my surprise.

"But look here, what do you mean?" said I. "What does Crawshay know about you?"

"Not much; but he suspects."

"Why should he?"

"Because, in his way he's very nearly as good a man as I am; because, my dear Bunny, with eyes in his head and brains behind them, he couldn't help suspecting. He saw me once in town with old Baird. He must have seen me that day in the pub. on the way to Milchester, as well as afterwards on the cricket-field. As a matter of fact, I know he did, for he wrote and told me so before his trial."

"He wrote to you! And you never told me!"

The old shrug answered the old grievance.

"What was the good, my dear fellow? It would only have worried you."

"Well, what did he say?"

"That he was sorry he had been run in before getting back to town, as he had proposed doing himself the honor of paying me a call; however, he trusted it was only a pleasure deferred, and he begged me not to go and get lagged myself before he came out. Of course he knew the Melrose necklace was gone, though he hadn't got it; and he said that the man who could take that and leave the rest was a man after his own heart. And so on, with certain little proposals for the far future, which I fear may be the very near future indeed! I'm only surprised he hasn't turned up yet."

He looked again towards the lobby, which he

had left in darkness, with the inner door shut as carefully as the outer one. I asked him what he meant to do.

"Let him knock—if he gets so far. The porter is to say I'm out of town; it will be true, too, in another hour or so."

"You're going off to-night?"

"By the 7.15 from Liverpool Street. I don't say much about my people, Bunny, but I have the best of sisters married to a country parson in the eastern counties. They always make me welcome, and let me read the lessons for the sake of getting me to church. I'm sorry you won't be there to hear me on Sunday, Bunny. I've figured out some of my best schemes in that parish, and I know of no better port in a storm. But I must pack. I thought I'd just let you know where I was going, and why, in case you cared to follow my example."

He flung the stump of his cigarette into the fire, stretched himself as he rose, and remained so long in the inelegant attitude that my eyes mounted from his body to his face; a second later they had followed his eyes across the room, and I also was on my legs. On the threshold of the folding doors that divided bedroom and sitting-room, a well-built man stood in ill-fitting broadcloth, and bowed to us until his bullet head presented an unbroken disk of short red hair.

Brief as was my survey of this astounding apparition, the interval was long enough for Raffles to recover his composure; his hands were in his pockets, and a smile upon his face, when my eyes flew back to him.

"Let me introduce you, Bunny," said he, "to our distinguished colleague, Mr. Reginald Crawshay."

The bullet head bobbed up, and there was a wrinkled brow above the coarse, shaven face, crimson also, I remember, from the grip of a collar several sizes too small. But I noted nothing consciously at the time. I had jumped to my own conclusion, and I turned on Raffles with an oath.

"It's a trick!" I cried. "It's another of your cursed tricks! You got him here, and then you got me. You want me to join you, I suppose? I'll see you damned!"

So cold was the stare which met this outburst that I became ashamed of my words while they were yet upon my lips.

"Really, Bunny!" said Raffles, and turned his shoulder with a shrug.

"Lord love yer," cried Crawshay, "'e knew nothin'. 'E didn't expect me; 'e's all right. And

you're the cool canary, *you* are," he went on to
Raffles. "I knoo you were, but, do me proud,
you're one after my own kidney!" And he thrust
out a shaggy hand.

"After that," said Raffles, taking it, "what am
I to say? But you must have heard my opinion
of you. I am proud to make your acquaintance.
How the deuce did you get in?"

"Never you mind," said Crawshay, loosening
his collar; "let's talk about how I'm to get out.
Lord love yer, but that's better!" There was a
livid ring round his bull-neck, that he fingered ten-
derly. "Didn't know how much longer I might
have to play the gent," he explained; "didn't know
who you'd bring in."

"Drink whiskey and soda?" inquired Raffles,
when the convict was in the chair from which I
had leapt.

"No, I drink it neat," replied Crawshay, "but
I talk business first. You don't get over me like
that, Lor' love yer!"

"Well, then, what can I do for you?"

"You know without me tellin' you."

"Give it a name."

"Clean heels, then; that's what I want to show,
and I leaves the way to you. We're brothers in
arms, though I ain't armed this time. It ain't

necessary. You've too much sense. But brothers we are, and you'll see a brother through. Let's put it at that. You'll see me through in yer own way. I leaves it all to you."

His tone was rich with conciliation and concession; he bent over and tore a pair of button boots from his bare feet, which he stretched towards the fire, painfully uncurling his toes.

"I hope you take a larger size than them," said he. "I'd have had a see if you'd given me time. I wasn't in long afore you."

"And you won't tell me how you got in?"

"Wot's the use? I can't teach *you* nothin'. Besides, I want out. I want out of London, an' England, an' bloomin' Europe too. That's all I want of you, mister. I don't arst how *you* go on the job. You know w'ere I come from, 'cos I 'eard you say; you know w'ere I want to 'ead for, 'cos I've just told yer; the details I leaves entirely to you."

"Well," said Raffles, "we must see what can be done."

"We must," said Mr. Crawshay, and leaned back comfortably, and began twirling his stubby thumbs.

Raffles turned to me with a twinkle in his eye; but his forehead was scored with thought, and resolve mingled with resignation in the lines of his mouth. And he spoke exactly as though he and I were alone in the room.

"You seize the situation, Bunny? If our friend here is 'copped,' to speak his language, he means to 'blow the gaff' on you and me. He is considerate enough not to say so in so many words, but it's plain enough, and natural enough for that matter. I would do the same in his place. We had the bulge before; he has it now; it's perfectly fair. We must take on this job; we aren't in a position to refuse it; even if we were, I should take it on! Our friend is a great sportsman; he has got clear away from Dartmoor; it would be a thousand pities to let him go back. Nor shall he; not if I can think of a way of getting him abroad."

"Any way you like," murmured Crawshay, with his eyes shut. "I leaves the 'ole thing to you."

"But you'll have to wake up and tell us things."

"All right, mister; but I'm fair on the rocks for a sleep!"

And he stood up, blinking.

"Think you were traced to town?"

"Must have been."

"And here?"

"Not in this fog—not with any luck."

Raffles went into the bedroom, lit the gas there, and returned next minute.

"So you got in by the window?"

"That's about it."

"It was devilish smart of you to know which one; it beats me how you brought it off in daylight, fog or no fog! But let that pass. You don't think you were seen?"

"I don't think it, sir."

"Well, let's hope you are right. I shall reconnoitre and soon find out. And you'd better come too, Bunny, and have something to eat and talk it over."

As Raffles looked at me, I looked at Crawshay, anticipating trouble; and trouble brewed in his blank, fierce face, in the glitter of his startled eyes, in the sudden closing of his fists.

"And what's to become o' me?" he cried out with an oath.

"You wait here."

"No, you don't," he roared, and at a bound had his back to the door. "You don't get round me like that, you cuckoos!"

Raffles turned to me with a twitch of the shoulders.

"That's the worst of these professors," said he; "they never will use their heads. They see the pegs, and they mean to hit 'em; but that's all they do see and mean, and they think we're the same. No wonder we licked them last time!"

"Don't talk through yer neck," snarled the convict. "Talk out straight, curse you!"

"Right," said Raffles. "I'll talk as straight as you like. You say you put yourself in my hands— you leave it all to me—yet you don't trust me an inch! I know what's to happen if I fail. I accept the risk. I take this thing on. Yet you think I'm going straight out to give you away and make you give me away in my turn. You're a fool, Mr. Crawshay, though you have broken Dartmoor; you've got to listen to a better man, and obey him. I see you through in my own way, or not at all. I come and go as I like, and with whom I like, without your interference; you stay here and lie just as low as you know how, be as wise as your word, and leave the whole thing to me. If you won't—if you're fool enough not to trust me— there's the door. Go out and say what you like, and be damned to you!"

Crawshay slapped his thigh.

"That's talking!" said he. "Lord love yer, I know where I am when you talk like that. I'll trust yer. I know a man when he get's his tongue between his teeth; you're all right. I don't say

so much about this other gent, though I saw him
along with you on the job that time in the prov-
inces; but if he's a pal of yours, Mr. Raffles, he'll
be all right too. I only hope you gents ain't too
stony——"

And he touched his pockets with a rueful
face.

"I only went for their togs," said he. "You
never struck two such stony-broke cusses in yer
life!"

"That's all right," said Raffles. "We'll see you
through properly. Leave it to us, and you sit
tight."

"Rightum!" said Crawshay. "And I'll have a
sleep time you're gone. But no sperrits—no,
thank'ee—not yet! Once let me loose on the lush,
and, Lord love yer, I'm a gone coon!"

Raffles got his overcoat, a long, light driving-
coat, I remember, and even as he put it on our
fugitive was dozing in the chair; we left him mur-
muring incoherently, with the gas out, and his bare
feet toasting.

"Not such a bad chap, that professor," said
Raffles on the stairs; "a real genius in his way, too,
though his methods are a little elementary for my
taste. But technique isn't everything; to get out
of Dartmoor and into the Albany in the same

twenty-four hours is a whole that justifies its parts. Good Lord!"

We had passed a man in the foggy courtyard, and Raffles had nipped my arm.

"Who was it?"

"The last man we want to see! I hope to heaven he didn't hear me!"

"But who is he, Raffles?"

"Our old friend Mackenzie, from the Yard!"

I stood still with horror.

"Do you think he's on Crawshay's track?"

"I don't know. I'll find out."

And before I could remonstrate he had wheeled me round; when I found my voice he merely laughed, and whispered that the bold course was the safe one every time.

"But it's madness——"

"Not it. Shut up! Is that *you*, Mr. Mackenzie?"

The detective turned about and scrutinized us keenly; and through the gaslit mist I noticed that his hair was grizzled at the temples, and his face still cadaverous, from the wound that had nearly been his death.

"Ye have the advantage o' me, sirs," said he.

"I hope you're fit again," said my companion.

The Amateur Cracksman

"My name is Raffles, and we met at Milchester last year."

"Is that a fact?" cried the Scotchman, with quite a start. "Yes, now I remember your face, and yours too, sir. Ay, yon was a bad business, but it ended vera well, an' that's the main thing."

His native caution had returned to him. Raffles pinched my arm.

"Yes, it ended splendidly, but for you," said he. "But what about this escape of the leader of the gang, that fellow Crawshay? What do you think of that, eh?"

"I havena the parteeculars," replied the Scot.

"Good!" cried Raffles. "I was only afraid you might be on his tracks once more!"

Mackenzie shook his head with a dry smile, and wished us good evening as an invisible window was thrown up, and a whistle blown softly through the fog.

"We must see this out," whispered Raffles. "Nothing more natural than a little curiosity on our part. After him, quick!"

And we followed the detective into another entrance on the same side as that from which we had emerged, the left-hand side on one's way to Piccadilly; quite openly we followed him, and at the foot of the stairs met one of the porters of the place. Raffles asked him what was wrong.

"Nothing, sir," said the fellow glibly.

"Rot!" said Raffles. "That was Mackenzie, the detective. I've just been speaking to him. What's he here for? Come on, my good fellow; we won't give you away, if you've instructions not to tell."

The man looked quaintly wistful, the temptation of an audience hot upon him; a door shut upstairs, and he fell.

"It's like this," he whispered. "This afternoon a gen'leman comes arfter rooms, and I sent him to the orfice; one of the clurks, 'e goes round with 'im an' shows 'im the empties, an' the gen'leman's partic'ly struck on the set the coppers is up in now. So he sends the clurk to fetch the manager, as there was one or two things he wished to speak about; an' when they come back, blowed if the gent isn't gone! Beg yer pardon, sir, but he's clean disappeared off the face o' the premises!" And the porter looked at us with shining eyes.

"Well?" said Raffles.

"Well, sir, they looked about, an' looked about, an' at larst they give him up for a bad job; thought he'd changed his mind an' didn't want to tip the clurk; so they shut up the place an' come away.

An' that's all till about 'alf an hour ago, when I takes the manager his extry-speshul *Star;* in about ten minutes he comes running out with a note, an' sends me with it to Scotland Yard in a hansom. An' that's all I know, sir—straight. The coppers is up there now, and the tec, and the manager, and they think their gent is about the place somewhere still. Least, I reckon that's their idea; but who he is, or what they want him for, I dunno."

"Jolly interesting!" said Raffles. "I'm going up to inquire. Come on, Bunny; there should be some fun."

"Beg yer pardon, Mr. Raffles, but you won't say nothing about me?"

"Not I; you're a good fellow. I won't forget it if this leads to sport. Sport!" he whispered as we reached the landing. "It looks like precious poor sport for you and me, Bunny!"

"What are you going to do?"

"I don't know. There's no time to think. This, to start with."

And he thundered on the shut door; a policeman opened it. Raffles strode past him with the air of a chief commissioner, and I followed before the man had recovered from his astonishment. The bare boards rang under us; in the bedroom we found a knot of officers stooping over the window-ledge with a constable's lantern. Mackenzie was the first to stand upright, and he greeted us with a glare.

"May I ask what you gentlemen want?" said he.

"We want to lend a hand," said Raffles briskly. "We lent one once before, and it was my friend here who took over from you the fellow who split on all the rest, and held him tightly. Surely that entitles him, at all events, to see any fun that's going? As for myself, well, it's true I only helped to carry you to the house; but for old acquaintance I do hope, my dear Mr. Mackenzie, that you will permit us to share such sport as there may be. I myself can only stop a few minutes, in any case."

"Then ye'll not see much," growled the detective, "for he's not up here. Constable, go you and stand at the foot o' the stairs, and let no other body come up on any conseederation; these gentlemen may be able to help us after all."

"That's kind of you, Mackenzie!" cried Raffles warmly. "But what is it all? I questioned a porter I met coming down, but could get nothing out of him, except that somebody had been to see these rooms and not since been seen himself."

The Amateur Cracksman

"He's a man we want," said Mackenzie. "He's concealed himself somewhere about these premises, or I'm vera much mistaken. D'ye reside in the Albany, Mr. Raffles?"

"I do."

"Will your rooms be near these?"

"On the next staircase but one."

"Ye'll just have left them?"

"Just."

"Been in all the afternoon, likely?"

"Not all."

"Then I may have to search your rooms, sir. I am prepared to search every room in the Albany! Our man seems to have gone for the leads; but unless he's left more marks outside than in, or we find him up there, I shall have the entire building to ransack."

"I will leave you my key," said Raffles at once. "I am dining out, but I'll leave it with the officer down below."

I caught my breath in mute amazement. What was the meaning of this insane promise? It was wilful, gratuitous, suicidal; it made me catch at his sleeve in open horror and disgust; but, with a word of thanks, Mackenzie had returned to his window-sill, and we sauntered unwatched through the folding-doors into the adjoining room. Here the window looked down into the courtyard; it was still open; and as we gazed out in apparent idleness, Raffles reassured me.

"It's all right, Bunny; you do what I tell you and leave the rest to me. It's a tight corner, but I don't despair. What you've got to do is to stick to these chaps, especially if they search my rooms; they mustn't poke about more than necessary, and they won't if you're there."

"But where will you be? You're never going to leave me to be landed alone?"

"If I do, it will be to turn up trumps at the right moment. Besides, there are such things as windows, and Crawshay's the man to take his risks. You must trust me, Bunny; you've known me long enough."

"Are you going now?"

"There's no time to lose. Stick to them, old chap; don't let them suspect *you,* whatever else you do." His hand lay an instant on my shoulder; then he left me at the window, and recrossed the room.

"I've got to go now," I heard him say; "but my friend will stay and see this through, and I'll leave the gas on in my rooms, and my key with the constable downstairs. Good luck, Mackenzie; only wish I could stay."

The Amateur Cracksman

"Good-by, sir," came in a preoccupied voice, "and many thanks."

Mackenzie was still busy at his window, and I remained at mine, a prey to mingled fear and wrath, for all my knowledge of Raffles and of his infinite resource. By this time I felt that I knew more or less what he would do in any given emergency; at least I could conjecture a characteristic course of equal cunning and audacity. He would return to his rooms, put Crawshay on his guard, and—stow him away? No—there were such things as windows. Then why was Raffles going to desert us all? I thought of many things—lastly of a cab. These bedroom windows looked into a narrow side-street; they were not very high; from them a man might drop on to the roof of a cab— even as it passed—and be driven away even under the noses of the police! I pictured Raffles driving that cab, unrecognizable in the foggy night; the vision came to me as he passed under the window, tucking up the collar of his great driving-coat on the way to his rooms; it was still with me when he passed again on his way back, and stopped to hand the constable his key.

"We're on his track," said a voice behind me. "He's got up on the leads, sure enough, though how he managed it from yon window is a myst'ry

The Return Match

to me. We're going to lock up here and try what like it is from the attics. So you'd better come with us if you've a mind."

The top floor at the Albany, as elsewhere, is devoted to the servants—a congeries of little kitchens and cubicles, used by many as lumber-rooms—by Raffles among the many. The annex in this case was, of course, empty as the rooms below; and that was lucky, for we filled it, what with the manager, who now joined us, and another tenant whom he brought with him to Mackenzie's undisguised annoyance.

"Better let in all Piccadilly at a crown a head," said he. "Here, my man, out you go on the roof to make one less, and have your truncheon handy."

We crowded to the little window, which Mackenzie took care to fill; and a minute yielded no sound but the crunch and slither of constabulary boots upon sooty slates. Then came a shout.

"What now?" cried Mackenzie.

"A rope," we heard, "hanging from the spout by a hook!"

"Sirs," purred Mackenzie, "yon's how he got up from below! He would do it with one o' they telescope sticks, an' I never thocht o't! How long a rope, my lad?"

"Quite short. I've got it."

The Amateur Cracksman

"Did it hang over a window? Ask him that!" cried the manager. "He can see by leaning over the parapet."

The question was repeated by Mackenzie; a pause, then "Yes, it did."

"Ask him how many windows along!" shouted the manager in high excitement.

"Six, he says," said Mackenzie next minute; and he drew in his head and shoulders. "I should just like to see those rooms, six windows along."

"Mr. Raffles," announced the manager after a mental calculation.

"Is that a fact?" cried Mackenzie. "Then we shall have no difficulty at all. He's left me his key down below."

The words had a dry, speculative intonation, which even then I found time to dislike; it was as though the coincidence had already struck the Scotchman as something more.

"Where is Mr. Raffles?" asked the manager, as we all filed downstairs.

"He's gone out to his dinner," said Mackenzie.

"Are you sure?"

"I saw him go," said I. My heart was beating horribly. I would not trust myself to speak again. But I wormed my way to a front place in the little procession, and was, in fact, the second man to cross the threshold that had been the Rubicon of my life. As I did so I uttered a cry of pain, for Mackenzie had trod back heavily on my toes; in another second I saw the reason, and saw it with another and a louder cry.

A man was lying at full length before the fire on his back, with a little wound in the white forehead, and the blood draining into his eyes. And the man was Raffles himself!

"Suicide," said Mackenzie calmly. "No—here's the poker—looks more like murder." He went on his knees and shook his head quite cheerfully. "An' it's not even murder," said he, with a shade of disgust in his matter-of-fact voice; "yon's no more than a flesh-wound, and I have my doubts whether it felled him; but, sirs, he just stinks o' chloryform!"

He got up and fixed his keen gray eyes upon me; my own were full of tears, but they faced him unashamed.

"I understood ye to say ye saw him go out?" said he sternly.

"I saw that long driving-coat; of course, I thought he was inside it."

"And I could ha' sworn it was the same gent when he give me the key!"

It was the disconsolate voice of the constable

in the background; on him turned Mackenzie, white to the lips.

"You'd think anything, some of you damned policemen," said he. "What's your number, you rotter? P 34? You'll be hearing more of this, Mr. P 34! If that gentleman was dead—instead of coming to himself while I'm talking—do you know what you'd be? Guilty of his manslaughter, you stuck pig in buttons! Do you know who you've let slip, butter-fingers? Crawshay—no less —him that broke Dartmoor yesterday. By the God that made ye, P 34, if I lose him I'll hound ye from the forrce!"

Working face—shaking fist—a calm man on fire. It was a new side of Mackenzie, and one to mark and to digest. Next moment he had flounced from our midst.

"Difficult thing to break your own head," said Raffles later; "infinitely easier to cut your own throat. Chloroform's another matter; when you've used it on others, you know the dose to a nicety. So you thought I was really gone? Poor old Bunny! But I hope Mackenzie saw your face?"

"He did," said I. I would not tell him all Mackenzie must have seen, however.

The Return Match

"That's all right. I wouldn't have had him miss it for worlds; and you mustn't think me a brute, old boy, for I fear that man, and, know, we sink or swim together."

"And now we sink or swim with Crawshay, too," said I dolefully.

"Not we!" said Raffles with conviction. "Old Crawshay's a true sportsman, and he'll do by us as we've done by him; besides, this makes us quits; and I don't think, Bunny, that we'll take on the professors again!"

The Gift of the Emperor

I

WHEN the King of the Cannibal Islands made faces at Queen Victoria, and a European monarch set the cables tingling with his compliments on the exploit, the indignation in England was not less than the surprise, for the thing was not so common as it has since become. But when it transpired that a gift of peculiar significance was to follow the congratulations, to give them weight, the inference prevailed that the white potentate and the black had taken simultaneous leave of their fourteen senses. For the gift was a pearl of price unparalleled, picked aforetime by British cutlasses from a Polynesian setting, and presented by British royalty to the sovereign who seized this opportunity of restoring it to its original possessor.

The incident would have been a godsend to the Press a few weeks later. Even in June there were leaders, letters, large headlines, leaded type; the *Daily Chronicle* devoting half its literary page to

The Gift of the Emperor

a charming drawing of the island capital which the new *Pall Mall,* in a leading article headed by a pun, advised the Government to blow to flinders. I was myself driving a poor but not dishonest quill at the time, and the topic of the hour goaded me into satiric verse which obtained a better place than anything I had yet turned out. I had let my flat in town, and taken inexpensive quarters at Thames Ditton, on the plea of a disinterested passion for the river.

"First-rate, old boy!" said Raffles (who must needs come and see me there), lying back in the boat while I sculled and steered. "I suppose they pay you pretty well for these, eh?"

"Not a penny."

"Nonsense, Bunny! I thought they paid so well? Give them time, and you'll get your check."

"Oh, no, I sha'n't," said I gloomily. "I've got to be content with the honor of getting in; the editor wrote to say so, in so many words," I added. But I gave the gentleman his distinguished name.

"You don't mean to say you've written for payment already?"

No; it was the last thing I had intended to admit. But I had done it. The murder was out; there was no sense in further concealment. I had

The Amateur Cracksman

written for my money because I really needed it;
if he must know, I was cursedly hard up. Raffles
nodded as though he knew already. I warmed to
my woes. It was no easy matter to keep your end
up as a raw freelance of letters; for my part, I
was afraid I wrote neither well enough nor ill
enough for success. I suffered from a persistent
ineffectual feeling after style. Verse I could manage; but it did not pay. To personal paragraphs
and the baser journalism I could not and I would
not stoop.

Raffles nodded again, this time with a smile that
stayed in his eyes as he leant back watching me.
I knew that he was thinking of other things I had
stooped to, and I thought I knew what he was
going to say. He had said it before so often; he
was sure to say it again. I had my answer ready,
but evidently he was tired of asking the same question. His lids fell, he took up the paper he had
dropped, and I sculled the length of the old red
wall of Hampton Court before he spoke again.

"And they gave you nothing for these! My
dear Bunny, they're capital, not only *qua* verses
but for crystallizing your subject and putting it in
a nutshell. Certainly you've taught *me* more
about it than I knew before. But is it really worth
fifty thousand pounds—a single pearl?"

The Gift of the Emperor

"A hundred, I believe; but that wouldn't scan."

"A hundred thousand pounds!" said Raffles, with his eyes shut. And again I made certain what was coming, but again I was mistaken. "If it's worth all that," he cried at last, "there would be no getting rid of it at all; it's not like a diamond that you can subdivide. But I beg your pardon, Bunny. I was forgetting!"

And we said no more about the emperor's gift; for pride thrives on an empty pocket, and no privation would have drawn from me the proposal which I had expected Raffles to make. My expectation had been half a hope, though I only knew it now. But neither did we touch again on what Raffles professed to have forgotten—my "apostasy," my "lapse into virtue," as he had been pleased to call it. We were both a little silent, a little constrained, each preoccupied with his own thoughts. It was months since we had met, and, as I saw him off towards eleven o'clock that Sunday night, I fancied it was for more months that we were saying good-by.

But as we waited for the train I saw those clear eyes peering at me under the station lamps, and when I met their glance Raffles shook his head.

"You don't look well on it, Bunny," said he.

"I never did believe in this Thames Valley. You want a change of air."

I wished I might get it.

"What you really want is a sea voyage."

"And a winter at St. Moritz, or do you recommend Cannes or Cairo? It's all very well, A. J., but you forget what I told you about my funds."

"I forget nothing. I merely don't want to hurt your feelings. But, look here, a sea voyage you shall have. I want a change myself, and you shall come with me as my guest. We'll spend July in the Mediterranean."

"But you're playing cricket——"

"Hang the cricket!"

"Well, if I thought you meant it——"

"Of course I mean it. Will you come?"

"Like a shot—if you go."

And I shook his hand, and waved mine in farewell, with the perfectly good-humored conviction that I should hear no more of the matter. It was a passing thought, no more, no less. I soon wished it were more; that week found me wishing myself out of England for good and all. I was making nothing. I could but subsist on the difference between the rent I paid for my flat and the rent at which I had sublet it, furnished, for the

The Gift of the Emperor

season. And the season was near its end, and creditors awaited me in town. Was it possible to be entirely honest? I had run no bills when I had money in my pocket, and the more downright dishonesty seemed to me the less ignoble.

But from Raffles, of course, I heard nothing more; a week went by, and half another week; then, late on the second Wednesday night, I found a telegram from him at my lodgings, after seeking him vainly in town, and dining with desperation at the solitary club to which I still belonged.

"Arrange to leave Waterloo by North German Lloyd special," he wired, "9.25 A. M. Monday next will meet you Southampton aboard *Uhlan* with tickets am writing."

And write he did, a light-hearted letter enough, but full of serious solicitude for me and for my health and prospects; a letter almost touching in the light of our past relations, in the twilight of their complete rupture. He said that he had booked two berths to Naples, that we were bound for Capri, which was clearly the island of the Lotos-eaters, that we would bask there together, "and for a while forget." It was a charming letter. I had never seen Italy; the privilege of initiation should be his. No mistake was greater than to deem it an impossible country for the summer.

The Amateur Cracksman

The Bay of Naples was never so divine, and he
wrote of "faëry lands forlorn," as though the
poetry sprang unbidden to his pen. To come back
to earth and prose, I might think it unpatriotic of
him to choose a German boat, but on no other line
did you receive such attention and accommodation
for your money. There was a hint of better reasons. Raffles wrote, as he had telegraphed, from
Bremen; and I gathered that the personal use of
some little influence with the authorities there had
resulted in a material reduction in our fares.

Imagine my excitement and delight! I managed to pay what I owed at Thames Ditton, to
squeeze a small editor for a very small check, and
my tailors for one more flannel suit. I remember
that I broke my last sovereign to get a box of Sullivan's cigarettes for Raffles to smoke on the voyage. But my heart was as light as my purse on
the Monday morning, the fairest morning of an
unfair summer, when the special whirled me
through the sunshine to the sea.

A tender awaited us at Southampton. Raffles
was not on board, nor did I really look for him
till we reached the liner's side. And then I looked
in vain. His face was not among the many that
fringed the rail; his hand was not of the few that
waved to friends. I climbed aboard in a sudden

The Gift of the Emperor

heaviness. I had no ticket, nor the money to pay for one. I did not even know the number of my room. My heart was in my mouth as I waylaid a steward and asked if a Mr. Raffles was on board. Thank heaven—he was! But where? The man did not know, was plainly on some other errand, and a-hunting I must go. But there was no sign of him on the promenade deck, and none below in the saloon; the smoking-room was empty but for a little German with a red moustache twisted into his eyes; nor was Raffles in his own cabin, whither I inquired my way in desperation, but where the sight of his own name on the baggage was certainly a further reassurance. Why he himself kept in the background, however, I could not conceive, and only sinister reasons would suggest themselves in explanation.

"So there you are! I've been looking for you all over the ship!"

Despite the graven prohibition, I had tried the bridge as a last resort; and there, indeed, was A. J. Raffles, seated on a skylight, and leaning over one of the officers' long chairs, in which reclined a girl in a white drill coat and skirt—a slip of a girl with a pale skin, dark hair, and rather remarkable eyes. So much I noted as he rose and quickly turned; thereupon I could think of nothing but the swift grimace which preceded a start of well-feigned astonishment.

"Why——*Bunny?*" cried Raffles. "Where have *you* sprung from?"

I stammered something as he pinched my hand.

"And are you coming in this ship? And to Naples, too? Well, upon my word! Miss Werner, may I introduce him?"

And he did so without a blush, describing me as an old schoolfellow whom he had not seen for months, with wilful circumstance and gratuitous detail that filled me at once with confusion, suspicion, and revolt. I felt myself blushing for us both, and I did not care. My address utterly deserted me, and I made no effort to recover it, to carry the thing off. All I would do was to mumble such words as Raffles actually put into my mouth, and that I doubt not with a thoroughly evil grace.

"So you saw my name in the list of passengers and came in search of me? Good old Bunny; I say, though, I wish you'd share my cabin. I've got a beauty on the promenade deck, but they wouldn't promise to keep me by myself. We ought to see about it before they shove in some alien. In any case we shall have to get out of this."

For a quartermaster had entered the wheel-

The Gift of the Emperor

house, and even while we had been speaking the pilot had taken possession of the bridge; as we descended, the tender left us with flying handkerchiefs and shrill good-bys; and as we bowed to Miss Werner on the promenade deck, there came a deep, slow throbbing under-foot, and our voyage had begun.

It did not begin pleasantly between Raffles and me. On deck he had overborne my stubborn perplexity by dint of a forced though forceful joviality; in his cabin the gloves were off.

"You idiot," he snarled, "you've given me away again!"

"How have I given you away?"

I ignored the separate insult in his last word.

"How? I should have thought any clod could see that I meant us to meet by chance!"

"After taking both tickets yourself?"

"They knew nothing about that on board; besides, I hadn't decided when I took the tickets."

"Then you should have let me know when you did decide. You lay your plans, and never say a word, and expect me to tumble to them by light of nature. How was I to know you had anything on?"

The Amateur Cracksman

I had turned the tables with some effect. Raffles almost hung his head.

"The fact is, Bunny, I didn't mean you to know. You—you've grown such a pious rabbit in your old age!"

My nickname and his tone went far to mollify me, other things went farther, but I had much to forgive him still.

"If you were afraid of writing," I pursued, "it was your business to give me the tip the moment I set foot on board. I would have taken it all right. I am not so virtuous as all that."

Was it my imagination, or did Raffles look slightly ashamed? If so, it was for the first and last time in all the years I knew him; nor can I swear to it even now.

"That," said he, "was the very thing I meant to do—to lie in wait in my room and get you as you passed. But——"

"You were better engaged?"

"Say otherwise."

"The charming Miss Werner?"

"She is quite charming."

"Most Australian girls are," said I.

"How did you know she was one?" he cried.

"I heard her speak."

"Brute!" said Raffles, laughing; "she has no

214

The Gift of the Emperor

more twang than you have. Her people are German, she has been to school in Dresden, and is on her way out alone."

"Money?" I inquired.

"Confound you!" he said, and, though he was laughing, I thought it was a point at which the subject might be changed.

"Well," I said, "it wasn't for Miss Werner you wanted us to play strangers, was it? You have some deeper game than that, eh?"

"I suppose I have."

"Then hadn't you better tell me what it is?"

Raffles treated me to the old cautious scrutiny that I knew so well; the very familiarity of it, after all these months, set me smiling in a way that might have reassured him; for dimly already I divined his enterprise.

"It won't send you off in the pilot's boat, Bunny?"

"Not quite."

"Then—you remember the pearl you wrote the——"

I did not wait for him to finish his sentence.

"You've got it!" I cried, my face on fire, for I caught sight of it that moment in the stateroom mirror.

Raffles seemed taken aback.

"Not yet," said he; "but I mean to have it before we get to Naples."

"Is it on board?"

"Yes."

"But how—where—who's got it?"

"A little German officer, a whipper-snapper with perpendicular mustaches."

"I saw him in the smoke-room."

"That's the chap; he's always there. Herr Captain Wilhelm von Heumann, if you look in the list. Well, he's the special envoy of the emperor, and he's taking the pearl out with him."

"You found this out in Bremen?"

"No, in Berlin, from a newspaper man I know there. I'm ashamed to tell you, Bunny, that I went there on purpose!"

I burst out laughing.

"You needn't be ashamed. You are doing the very thing I was rather hoping you were going to propose the other day on the river."

"You were *hoping* it?" said Raffles, with his eyes wide open. Indeed, it was his turn to show surprise, and mine to be much more ashamed than I felt.

"Yes," I answered, "I was quite keen on the idea, but I wasn't going to propose it."

The Gift of the Emperor

"Yet you would have listened to me the other day?"

Certainly I would, and I told him so without reserve; not brazenly, you understand; not even now with the gusto of a man who savors such an adventure for its own sake, but doggedly, defiantly, through my teeth, as one who had tried to live honestly and failed. And, while I was about it, I told him much more. Eloquently enough, I daresay, I gave him chapter and verse of my hopeless struggle, my inevitable defeat; for hopeless and inevitable they were to a man with my record, even though that record was written only in one's own soul. It was the old story of the thief trying to turn honest man; the thing was against nature, and there was an end of it.

Raffles entirely disagreed with me. He shook his head over my conventional view. Human nature was a board of checkers; why not reconcile one's self to alternate black and white? Why desire to be all one thing or all the other, like our forefathers on the stage or in the old-fashioned fiction? For his part, he enjoyed himself on all squares of the board, and liked the light the better for the shade. My conclusion he considered absurd.

"But you err in good company, Bunny, for all

the cheap moralists who preach the same twaddle: old Virgil was the first and worst offender of you all. I back myself to climb out of Avernus any day I like, and sooner or later I shall climb out for good. I suppose I can't very well turn myself into a Limited Liability Company. But I could retire and settle down and live blamelessly ever after. I'm not sure that it couldn't be done on this pearl alone!"

"Then you don't still think it too remarkable to sell?"

"We might take a fishery and haul it up with smaller fry. It would come after months of ill luck, just as we were going to sell the schooner; by Jove, it would be the talk of the Pacific!"

"Well, we've got to get it first. Is this von What's-his-name a formidable cuss?"

"More so than he looks; and he has the cheek of the devil!"

As he spoke a white drill skirt fluttered past the open state-room door, and I caught a glimpse of an upturned moustache beyond.

"But is he the chap we have to deal with? Won't the pearl be in the purser's keeping?"

Raffles stood at the door, frowning out upon the Solent, but for an instant he turned to me with a sniff.

The Gift of the Emperor

"My good fellow, do you suppose the whole ship's company knows there's a gem like that aboard? You said that it was worth a hundred thousand pounds; in Berlin they say it's priceless. I doubt if the skipper himself knows that von Heumann has it on him."

"And he has?"

"Must have."

"Then we have only him to deal with?"

He answered me without a word. Something white was fluttering past once more, and Raffles, stepping forth, made the promenaders three.

II

I do not ask to set foot aboard a finer steamship than the *Uhlan* of the Norddeutscher Lloyd, to meet a kindlier gentleman than her commander, or better fellows than his officers. This much at least let me have the grace to admit. I hated the voyage. It was no fault of anybody connected with the ship; it was no fault of the weather, which was monotonously ideal. Not even in my own heart did the reason reside; conscience and I were divorced at last, and the decree made absolute.

The Amateur Cracksman

With my scruples had fled all fear, and I was ready
to revel between bright skies and sparkling sea
with the light-hearted detachment of Raffles himself. It was Raffles himself who prevented me,
but not Raffles alone. It was Raffles and that
Colonial minx on her way home from school.

What he could see in her—but that begs the
question. Of course he saw no more than I did,
but to annoy me, or perhaps to punish me for my
long defection, he must turn his back on me and
devote himself to this chit from Southampton to
the Mediterranean. They were always together.
It was too absurd. After breakfast they would
begin, and go on until eleven or twelve at night;
there was no intervening hour at which you might
not hear her nasal laugh, or his quiet voice talking
soft nonsense into her ear. Of course it was nonsense! Is it conceivable that a man like Raffles,
with his knowledge of the world, and his experience of women (a side of his character upon
which I have purposely never touched, for it deserves another volume); is it credible, I ask, that
such a man could find anything but nonsense to talk
by the day together to a giddy young schoolgirl?
I would not be unfair for the world. I think I
have admitted that the young person had points.
Her eyes, I suppose, were really fine, and certainly

The Gift of the Emperor

the shape of the little brown face was charming, so far as mere contour can charm. I admit also more audacity than I cared about, with enviable health, mettle, and vitality. I may not have occasion to report any of this young lady's speeches (they would scarcely bear it), and am therefore the more anxious to describe her without injustice. I confess to some little prejudice against her. I resented her success with Raffles, of whom, in consequence, I saw less and less each day. It is a mean thing to have to confess, but there must have been something not unlike jealousy rankling within me.

Jealousy there was in another quarter—crude, rampant, undignified jealousy. Captain von Heumann would twirl his mustaches into twin spires, shoot his white cuffs over his rings, and stare at me insolently through his rimless eyeglasses; we ought to have consoled each other, but we never exchanged a syllable. The captain had a murderous scar across one of his cheeks, a present from Heidelberg, and I used to think how he must long to have Raffles there to serve the same. It was not as though von Heumann never had his innings. Raffles let him go in several times a day, for the malicious pleasure of bowling him out as he was "getting set"; those were his words when I taxed him disingenuously with obnoxious conduct towards a German on a German boat.

"You'll make yourself disliked on board!"

"By von Huemann merely."

"But is that wise when he's the man we've got to diddle?"

"The wisest thing I ever did. To have chummed up with him would have been fatal—the common dodge."

I was consoled, encouraged, almost content. I had feared Raffles was neglecting things, and I told him so in a burst. Here we were near Gibraltar, and not a word since the Solent. He shook his head with a smile.

"Plenty of time, Bunny, plenty of time. We can do nothing before we get to Genoa, and that won't be till Sunday night. The voyage is still young, and so are we; let's make the most of things while we can."

It was after dinner on the promenade deck, and as Raffles spoke he glanced sharply fore and aft, leaving me next moment with a step full of purpose. I retired to the smoking-room, to smoke and read in a corner, and to watch von Huemann, who very soon came to drink beer and to sulk in another.

Few travellers tempt the Red Sea at midsummer;

The Gift of the Emperor

the *Uhlan* was very empty indeed. She had, however, but a limited supply of cabins on the promenade deck, and there was just that excuse for my sharing Raffles's room. I could have had one to myself downstairs, but I must be up above. Raffles had insisted that I should insist on the point. So we were together, I think, without suspicion, though also without any object that I could see.

On the Sunday afternoon I was asleep in my berth, the lower one, when the curtains were shaken by Raffles, who was in his shirt-sleeves on the settee.

"Achilles sulking in his bunk!"

"What else is there to do?" I asked him as I stretched and yawned. I noted, however, the good-humor of his tone, and did my best to catch it.

"I have found something else, Bunny."

"I daresay!"

"You misunderstand me. The whipper-snapper's making his century this afternoon. I've had other fish to fry."

I swung my legs over the side of my berth and sat forward, as he was sitting, all attention. The inner door, a grating, was shut and bolted, and curtained like the open porthole.

"We shall be at Genoa before sunset," continued

Raffles. "It's the place where the deed's got to be done."

"So you still mean to do it?"

"Did I ever say I didn't?"

"You have said so little either way."

"Advisedly so, my dear Bunny; why spoil a pleasure trip by talking unnecessary shop? But now the time has come. It must be done at Genoa or not at all."

"On land?"

"No, on board, to-morrow night. To-night would do, but to-morrow is better, in case of mishap. If we were forced to use violence we could get away by the earliest train, and nothing be known till the ship was sailing and von Heumann found dead or drugged——"

"Not dead!" I exclaimed.

"Of course not," assented Raffles, "or there would be no need for us to bolt; but if we should have to bolt, Tuesday morning is our time, when this ship has got to sail, whatever happens. But I don't anticipate any violence. Violence is a confession of terrible incompetence. In all these years how many blows have you known me to strike? Not one, I believe; but I have been quite ready to kill my man every time, if the worst came to the worst."

The Gift of the Emperor

I asked him how he proposed to enter von Heumann's state-room unobserved, and even through the curtained gloom of ours his face lighted up.

"Climb into my bunk, Bunny, and you shall see."

I did so, but could see nothing. Raffles reached across me and tapped the ventilator, a sort of trap-door in the wall above his bed, some eighteen inches long and half that height. It opened outwards into the ventilating shaft.

"That," said he, "is our door to fortune. Open it if you like; you won't see much, because it doesn't open far; but loosening a couple of screws will set that all right. The shaft, as you may see, is more or less bottomless; you pass under it whenever you go to your bath, and the top is a skylight on the bridge. That's why this thing has to be done while we're at Genoa, because they keep no watch on the bridge in port. The ventilator opposite ours is von Huemann's. It again will only mean a couple of screws, and there's a beam to stand on while you work."

"But if anybody should look up from below?"

"It's extremely unlikely that anybody will be astir below, so unlikely that we can afford to chance it. No, I can't have you there to make sure. The great point is that neither of us should be seen from the time we turn in. A couple of ship's boys do sentry-go on these decks, and they shall be our witnesses; by Jove, it'll be the biggest mystery that ever was made!"

"If von Heumann doesn't resist."

"Resist! He won't get the chance. He drinks too much beer to sleep light, and nothing is so easy as to chloroform a heavy sleeper; you've even done it yourself on an occasion of which it's perhaps unfair to remind you. Von Heumann will be past sensation almost as soon as I get my hand through his ventilator. I shall crawl in over his body, Bunny, my boy!"

"And I?"

You will hand me what I want and hold the fort in case of accidents, and generally lend me the moral support you've made me require. It's a luxury, Bunny, but I found it devilish difficult to do without it after you turned pi!"

He said that Von Heumann was certain to sleep with a bolted door, which he, of course, would leave unbolted, and spoke of other ways of laying a false scent while rifling the cabin. Not that Raffles anticipated a tiresome search. The pearl would be about von Huemann's person; in fact, Raffles knew exactly where and in what he kept it. Naturally I asked how he could have come by such knowledge, and his answer led up to a momentary unpleasantness.

"It's a very old story, Bunny. I really forget in what Book it comes; I'm only sure of the Testament. But Samson was the unlucky hero, and one Delilah the heroine."

And he looked so knowing that I could not be in a moment's doubt as to his meaning.

"So the fair Australian has been playing Delilah?" said I.

"In a very harmless, innocent sort of way."

"She got his mission out of him?"

"Yes, I've forced him to score all the points he could, and that was his great stroke, as I hoped it would be. He has even shown Amy the pearl."

"Amy, eh! and she promptly told you?"

"Nothing of the kind. What makes you think so? I had the greatest trouble in getting it out of her."

His tone should have been a sufficient warning to me. I had not the tact to take it as such. At last I knew the meaning of his furious flirtation, and stood wagging my head and shaking my finger, blinded to his frowns by my own enlightenment.

"Wily worm!" said I. "Now I see through it all; how dense I've been!"

"Sure you're not still?"

"No; now I understand what has beaten me all the week. I simply couldn't fathom what you saw in that little girl. I never dreamt it was part of the game."

"So you think it was that and nothing more?"

"You deep old dog—of course I do!"

"You didn't know she was the daughter of a wealthy squatter?"

"There are wealthy women by the dozen who would marry you to-morrow."

"It doesn't occur to you that I might like to draw stumps, start clean, and live happily ever after—in the bush?"

"With that voice? It certainly does not!"

"Bunny!" he cried, so fiercely that I braced myself for a blow.

But no more followed.

"Do you think you would live happily?" I made bold to ask him.

"God knows!" he answered. And with that he left me, to marvel at his look and tone, and, more than ever, at the insufficiently exciting cause.

The Gift of the Emperor

III

Of all the mere feats of cracksmanship which I have seen Raffles perform, at once the most delicate and most difficult was that which he accomplished between one and two o'clock on the Tuesday morning, aboard the North German steamer *Uhlan,* lying at anchor in Genoa harbor.

Not a hitch occurred. Everything had been foreseen; everything happened as I had been assured everything must. Nobody was about below, only the ship's boys on deck, and nobody on the bridge. It was twenty-five minutes past one when Raffles, without a stitch of clothing on his body, but with a glass phial, corked with cotton-wool, between his teeth, and a tiny screw-driver behind his ear, squirmed feet first through the ventilator over his berth; and it was nineteen minutes to two when he returned, head first, with the phial still between his teeth, and the cotton-wool rammed home to still the rattling of that which lay like a great gray bean within. He had taken screws out and put them in again; he had unfastened von Heumann's ventilator and had left it fast as he had found it—fast as he instantly proceeded to make his own. As for von Heumann, it had been enough to place the drenched wad first on his mustache, and then to hold it between his gaping lips; thereafter the intruder had climbed both ways across his shins without eliciting a groan.

And here was the prize—this pearl as large as a filbert—with a pale pink tinge like a lady's fingernail—this spoil of a filibustering age—this gift from a European emperor to a South Sea chief. We gloated over it when all was snug. We toasted it in whiskey and soda-water laid in overnight in view of the great moment. But the moment was greater, more triumphant, than our most sanguine dreams. All we had now to do was to secrete the gem (which Raffles had prised from its setting, replacing the latter), so that we could stand the strictest search and yet take it ashore with us at Naples; and this Raffles was doing when I turned in. I myself would have landed incontinently, that night, at Genoa and bolted with the spoil; he would not hear of it, for a dozen good reasons which will be obvious.

On the whole I do not think that anything was discovered or suspected before we weighed anchor; but I cannot be sure. It is difficult to believe that a man could be chloroformed in his sleep and feel no tell-tale effects, sniff no suspicious odor, in the morning. Nevertheless, von Heumann reappeared as though nothing had happened to him, his German cap over his eyes and his mustaches brushing the peak. And by ten o'clock we were quit of Genoa; the last lean, blue-chinned official had left our decks; the last fruitseller had been beaten off with bucketsful of water and left cursing us from his boat; the last passenger had come aboard at the last moment—a fussy graybeard who kept the big ship waiting while he haggled with his boatman over half a lira. But at length we were off, the tug was shed, the lighthouse passed, and Raffles and I leaned together over the rail, watching our shadows on the pale green, liquid, veined marble that again washed the vessel's side.

Von Heumann was having his innings once more; it was part of the design that he should remain in all day, and so postpone the inevitable hour; and, though the lady looked bored, and was for ever glancing in our direction, he seemed only too willing to avail himself of his opportunities. But Raffles was moody and ill-at-ease. He had not the air of a successful man. I could but opine that the impending parting at Naples sat heavily on his spirit.

He would neither talk to me, nor would he let me go.

"Stop where you are, Bunny. I've things to tell you. Can you swim?"

"A bit."

"Ten miles?"

"Ten?" I burst out laughing. "Not one! Why do you ask?"

"We shall be within a ten miles' swim of the shore most of the day."

"What on earth are you driving at, Raffles?"

"Nothing; only I shall swim for it if the worst comes to the worst. I suppose you can't swim under water at all?"

I did not answer his question. I scarcely heard it: cold beads were bursting through my skin.

"Why should the worst come to the worst?" I whispered. "We aren't found out, are we?"

"No."

"Then why speak as though we were?"

"We may be; an old enemy of ours is on board."

"An old enemy?"

"Mackenzie."

"Never!"

"The man with the beard who came aboard last."

"Are you sure?"

"Sure! I was only sorry to see you didn't recognize him too."

The Gift of the Emperor

I took my handkerchief to my face; now that I thought of it, there had been something familiar in the old man's gait, as well as something rather youthful for his apparent years; his very beard seemed unconvincing, now that I recalled it in the light of this horrible revelation. I looked up and down the deck, but the old man was nowhere to be seen.

"That's the worst of it," said Raffles. "I saw him go into the captain's cabin twenty minutes ago."

"But what can have brought him?" I cried miserably. "Can it be a coincidence—is it somebody else he's after?"

Raffles shook his head.

"Hardly this time."

"Then you think he's after you?"

"I've been afraid of it for some weeks."

"Yet there you stand!"

"What am I to do? I don't want to swim for it before I must. I begin to wish I'd taken your advice, Bunny, and left the ship at Genoa. But I've not the smallest doubt that Mac was watching both ship and station till the last moment. That's why he ran it so fine."

He took a cigarette and handed me the case, but I shook my head impatiently.

"I still don't understand," said I. "Why should

he be after you? He couldn't come all this way about a jewel which was perfectly safe for all he knew. What's your own theory?"

"Simply that he's been on my track for some time, probably ever since friend Crawshay slipped clean through his fingers last November. There have been other indications. I am really not unprepared for this. But it can only be pure suspicion. I'll defy him to bring anything home, and I'll defy him to find the pearl! Theory, my dear Bunny? I know how he's got here as well as though I'd been inside that Scotchman's skin, and I know what he'll do next. He found out I'd gone abroad, and looked for a motive; he found out about von Heumann and his mission, and there was his motive cut-and-dried. Great chance—to nab me on a new job altogether. But he won't do it, Bunny; mark my words, he'll search the ship and search us all, when the loss is known; but he'll search in vain. And there's the skipper beckoning the whipper-snapper to his cabin: the fat will be in the fire in five minutes!"

Yet there was no conflagration, no fuss, no searching of the passengers, no whisper of what had happened in the air; instead of a stir there was portentous peace; and it was clear to me that Raffles was not a little disturbed at the falsification of all his predictions. There was something sinister in silence under such a loss, and the silence was sustained for hours during which Mackenzie never reappeared. But he was abroad during the luncheon-hour—he was in our cabin! I had left my book in Raffles's berth, and in taking it after lunch I touched the quilt. It was warm from the recent pressure of flesh and blood, and on an instinct I sprang to the ventilator; as I opened it the ventilator opposite was closed with a snap.

I waylaid Raffles. "All right! Let him find the pearl."

"Have you dumped it overboard?"

"That's a question I shan't condescend to answer."

He turned on his heel, and at subsequent intervals I saw him making the most of his last afternoon with the inevitable Miss Werner. I remember that she looked both cool and smart in quite a simple affair of brown holland, which toned well with her complexion, and was cleverly relieved with touches of scarlet. I quite admired her that afternoon, for her eyes were really very good, and so were her teeth, yet I had never admired her more directly in my own despite. For I passed them again and again in order to get a word with Raffles, to tell him I knew there was danger in the wind;

but he would not so much as catch my eye. So at last I gave it up. And I saw him next in the captain's cabin.

They had summoned him first; he had gone in smiling; and smiling I found him when they summoned me. The state-room was spacious, as befitted that of a commander. Mackenzie sat on the settee, his beard in front of him on the polished table; but a revolver lay in front of the captain; and, when I had entered, the chief officer, who had summoned me, shut the door and put his back to it. Von Heumann completed the party, his fingers busy with his mustache.

Raffles greeted me.

"This is a great joke!" he cried. "You remember the pearl you were so keen about, Bunny, the emperor's pearl, the pearl money wouldn't buy? It seems it was entrusted to our little friend here, to take out to Canoodle Dum, and the poor little chap's gone and lost it; *ergo,* as we're Britishers, they think we've got it!"

"But I know ye have," put in Mackenzie, nodding to his beard.

"You will recognize that loyal and patriotic voice," said Raffles. "Mon, 'tis our auld acquaintance Mackenzie, o' Scoteland Yarrd an' Scoteland itsel' !"

The Gift of the Emperor

"Dat is enough," cried the captain. "Have you submid to be searge, or do I vorce you?"

"What you will," said Raffles, "but it will do you no harm to give us fair play first. You accuse us of breaking into Captain von Heumann's stateroom during the small hours of this morning, and abstracting from it this confounded pearl. Well, I can prove that I was in my own room all night long, and I have no doubt my friend can prove the same."

"Most certainly I can," said I indignantly. "The ship's boys can bear witness to that."

Mackenzie laughed, and shook his head at his reflection in the polished mahogany.

"That was ver clever," said he, "and like enough it would ha' served ye had I not stepped aboard. But I've just had a look at they ventilators, and I think I know how ye worrked it. Anyway, captain, it makes no matter. I'll just be clappin' the darbies on these young sparks, an' then——"

"By what right?" roared Raffles, in a ringing voice, and I never saw his face in such a blaze. "Search us if you like; search every scrap and stitch we possess; but you dare to lay a finger on us without a warrant!"

"I wouldna' dare," said Mackenzie, as he fumbled in his breast pocket, and Raffles dived his hand into his own. "Haud his wrist!" shouted the Scotchman; and the huge Colt that had been with us many a night, but had never been fired in my hearing, clattered on the table and was raked in by the captain.

"All right," said Raffles savagely to the mate. "You can let go now. I won't try it again. Now, Mackenzie, let's see your warrant!"

"Ye'll no mishandle it?"

"What good would that do me? Let me see it," said Raffles, peremptorily, and the detective obeyed. Raffles raised his eyebrows as he perused the document; his mouth hardened, but suddenly relaxed; and it was with a smile and a shrug that he returned the paper.

"Wull that do for ye?" inquired Mackenzie.

"It may. I congratulate you, Mackenzie; it's a strong hand, at any rate. Two burglaries and the Melrose necklace, Bunny!" And he turned to me with a rueful smile.

"An' all easy to prove," said the Scotchman, pocketing the warrant. "I've one o' these for you," he added, nodding to me, "only not such a long one."

"To think," said the captain reproachfully, "that my shib should be made a den of thiefs! It shall be a very disagreeable madder, I have been obliged to pud you both in irons until we get to Nables."

"Surely not!" exclaimed Raffles. "Mackenzie, intercede with him; don't give your countrymen away before all hands! Captain, we can't escape; surely you could hush it up for the night? Look here, here's everything I have in my pockets; you empty yours, too, Bunny, and they shall strip us stark if they suspect we've weapons up our sleeves. All I ask is that we are allowed to get out of this without gyves upon our wrists!"

"Webbons you may not have," said the captain; "but wad aboud der bearl dat you were sdealing?"

"You shall have it!" cried Raffles. "You shall have it this minute if you guarantee no public indignity on board!"

"That I'll see to," said Mackenzie, "as long as you behave yourselves. There now, where is't?"

"On the table under your nose."

My eyes fell with the rest, but no pearl was there; only the contents of our pockets—our watches, pocket-books, pencils, penknives, cigarette cases—lay on the shiny table along with the revolvers already mentioned.

"Ye're humbuggin' us," said Mackenzie. "What's the use?"

"I'm doing nothing of the sort," laughed Raffles. "I'm testing you. Where's the harm?"

"It's here, joke apart?"

"On that table, by all my gods."

Mackenzie opened the cigarette cases and shook each particular cigarette. Thereupon Raffles prayed to be allowed to smoke one, and, when his prayer was heard, observed that the pearl had been on the table much longer than the cigarettes. Mackenzie promptly caught up the Colt and opened the chamber in the butt.

"Not there, not there," said Raffles; "but you're getting hot. Try the cartridges."

Mackenzie emptied them into his palm, and shook each one at his ear without result.

"Oh, give them to me!"

And, in an instant, Raffles had found the right one, had bitten out the bullet, and placed the emperor's pearl with a flourish in the centre of the table.

"After that you will perhaps show me such little consideration as is in your power. Captain, I have been a bit of a villain, as you see, and as such I am ready and willing to lie in irons all night if you deem it requisite for the safety of the ship. All I ask is that you do me one favor first."

"That shall debend on wad der vafour has been."

The Gift of the Emperor

"Captain, I've done a worse thing aboard your ship than any of you know. I have become engaged to be married, and I want to say good-by!"

I suppose we were all equally amazed; but the only one to express his amazement was von Heumann, whose deep-chested German oath was almost his first contribution to the proceedings. He was not slow to follow it, however, with a vigorous protest against the proposed farewell; but he was overruled, and the masterful prisoner had his way. He was to have five minutes with the girl, while the captain and Mackenzie stood within range (but not earshot), with their revolvers behind their backs. As we were moving from the cabin, in a body, he stopped and gripped my hand.

"So I've let you in at last, Bunny—at last and after all! If you knew how sorry I am. . . . But you won't get much—I don't see why you should get anything at all. Can you forgive me? This may be for years, and it may be for ever, you know! You were a good pal always when it came to the scratch; some day or other you mayn't be so sorry to remember you were a good pal at the last!"

There was a meaning in his eye that I understood; and my teeth were set, and my nerve strung ready, as I wrung that strong and cunning hand for the last time in my life.

How that last scene stays with me, and will stay to my death! How I see every detail, every shadow on the sunlit deck! We were among the islands that dot the course from Genoa to Naples; that was Elba falling back on our starboard quarter, that purple patch with the hot sun setting over it. The captain's cabin opened to starboard, and the starboard promenade deck, sheeted with sunshine and scored with shadow, was deserted, but for the group of which I was one, and for the pale, slim, brown figure further aft with Raffles. Engaged? I could not believe it, cannot to this day. Yet there they stood together, and we did not hear a word; there they stood out against the sunset, and the long, dazzling highway of sunlit sea that sparkled from Elba to the *Uhlan's* plates; and their shadows reached almost to our feet.

Suddenly—an instant—and the thing was done —a thing I have never known whether to admire or to detest. He caught her—he kissed her before us all—then flung her from him so that she almost fell. It was that action which foretold the next. The mate sprang after him, and I sprang after the mate.

Raffles was on the rail, but only just.

The Gift of the Emperor

"Hold him, Bunny!" he cried. "Hold him tight!"

And, as I obeyed that last behest with all my might, without a thought of what I was doing, save that he bade me do it, I saw his hands shoot up and his head bob down, and his lithe, spare body cut the sunset as cleanly and precisely as though he had plunged at his leisure from a diver's board!

* * * * * *

Of what followed on deck I can tell you nothing, for I was not there. Nor can my final punishment, my long imprisonment, my everlasting disgrace, concern or profit you, beyond the interest and advantage to be gleaned from the knowledge that I at least had my deserts. But one thing I must set down, believe it who will—one more thing only and I am done.

It was into a second-class cabin, on the starboard side, that I was promptly thrust in irons, and the door locked upon me as though I were another Raffles. Meanwhile a boat was lowered, and the sea scoured to no purpose, as is doubtless on record elsewhere. But either the setting sun, flashing over the waves, must have blinded all eyes, or else mine were victims of a strange illusion.

For the boat was back, the screw throbbing, and the prisoner peering through his porthole across the sunlit waters that he believed had closed for ever over his comrade's head. Suddenly the sun sank behind the Island of Elba, the lane of dancing sunlight was instantaneously quenched and swallowed in the trackless waste, and in the middle distance, already miles astern, either my sight deceived me or a black speck bobbed amid the gray. The bugle had blown for dinner: it may well be that all save myself had ceased to strain an eye. And now I lost what I had found, now it rose, now sank, and now I gave it up utterly. Yet anon it would rise again, a mere mote dancing in the dim gray distance, drifting towards a purple island, beneath a fading western sky, streaked with dead gold and cerise. And night fell before I knew whether it was a human head or not.

THE END